A Bad Year For Trees & Other Stories

A Bad Year For Trees

& Other Stories

* * *

Catherine Czerkawska

Published by Dyrock Publishing

Copyright © 2022 Catherine Czerkawska

Cover image by Catherine Czerkawska

ISBN: 978-0-9557364-4-5

Contents

A Quiet Afternoon In
The Museum Of Torture

'Davy. Come and look at this.'

Her husband is loitering in another room, reading graphic descriptions of cruelty. Ros turns her attention back to the photograph of a real woman, naked except for the spiked metal contraption which doesn't seem to be troubling her at all. The woman stands there, plump and complacent, hands by her sides. It's an old photograph from the 1920s perhaps. She has long hair, a pretty face, a round belly. Ros wonders about the picture. Was it from a serious medical text or, more likely, one of those naughty postcards that gentlemen used to pass around for their private titillation? She remembers reading that most of the girls in those pictures were ruthlessly exploited by the photographers but this woman looks faintly bored if anything. Ros reads the caption.

'The chastity belt had very little to do with knights locking away their wives while they went off on Crusades. It was much more about women defending themselves against rape during times of siege or on dangerous journeys.'

Unlike the other exhibits, at least the chastity belt seems to have had a reasonable purpose. As for the rest, a miscellany of cruelty, how could so much ingenuity be dedicated to such dreadful ends? And why are so many of these things decorated? Why the intricate carving, the brilliant colours? Why go the length of making them so pretty?

She can hear her husband's footsteps, the characteristic jiggle of coins and keys in his pocket, but otherwise the museum is quiet. He comes up behind her and puts his hands on her shoulders while he looks at the chastity belt with its curved, outward-facing spikes.

'Ouch,' he says. 'That would set your gas at a peep, wouldn't it?' He peers more closely. 'Christ you wouldn't even want to have a wee feel, would you?'

'I think that's the general idea.'

It is an October afternoon in this small hill town in Tuscany. And it is raining. They were on their way to seek shelter in the Etruscan Museum when Davy was side-tracked by the sign advertising the *Museo Della Tortura* with a wooden cage containing a skeleton in the doorway.

'Oh wow,' he said. 'Come on. Let's go in.'

'But the baby ...'

'The baby's fast asleep. He won't know where he is. His world is one giant milk bar.'

It's true enough. Angus is asleep in his sling, his cheek turned towards her breast. He is too heavy for it now, a big boy, gaining weight fast, and her back hurts, but he seems so comfortable that she puts up with it for the sake of peace and quiet.

This is their first holiday as a family. Until now, it has always been just the two of them, exploring foreign cities, eating, drinking a bit too much wine, making love, making, as it turned out, a baby. Now, just getting away from home together seems like an achievement. She is tired all the time. She has to be careful what she eats because some foods upset the baby. And as for lovemaking ... she finds herself thinking of the chastity belt with approval.

'Don't you think he's a bit young for flying?' said her mother. But she put the baby discreetly to the breast for most of the journey. He suckled and slept, alternately. When they were getting off the plane, a woman peered over her shoulder.

'My God, such a new baby. How did you keep him so quiet?'

I just plugged him in, she thought, but instead she said, 'He's a good baby. A good boy.'

They have rented a small farmhouse on the edge of a hill village. Davy drives the hire car warily from Pisa along roads that are neither straight nor level, but elbow their way up and down hills at alarming angles.

'Well the Romans sure didn't build these.'

'Maybe it was the local boys.'

Davy grins. 'Do you smell burning clutch?'

She navigates while the baby sleeps, securely strapped in behind them. Ponsacco, La Streza, Laiatico. She checks off a litany of names, her finger on the map, tracing the bendy roads and the unfamiliar syllables.

'Do you know that Andrea Bocelli comes from La Streza?'

Davy shakes his head. 'Not a lot of people know that.'

The day is damp, the leaves beginning to tumble around them. All the colours are clear and deep. The light gets into her head and stays there. Back in Scotland, everything will seem subdued and subtle for weeks. The narrow road climbs through the village, between red-roofed houses, until they are almost out the other side, among the trees again. From the terrace of the villa they can see a hundred villages and towns and houses like this one, clinging to the tops of hills above layers of landscape with creamy clouds sandwiched between.

The villa is clean with white painted walls and shiny terracotta floors. 'Thank God,' she thinks, with the baby on her mind. There is a playroom with toys, the kitchen cupboards have olive oil, balsamic vinegar, packets of pasta left by previous occupants. The bathroom has shampoo and shower gel and a large centipede who lives behind the gas boiler and ventures out infrequently to inspect the visitors.

The place is festooned with handwritten notes from the housekeeper.

'When you return to your house, you leave rubbish in the house because cats make a hole in bags.'

'No deliver this key to any place.'

'This is a kit of first aid when necessary.'

There are bookshelves stuffed with novels in bright covers, books with titles in which words like sun, summer, lemons, and the inevitable Tuscany figure prominently. She flicks through them, nursing the baby, a cooling cup of tea at her side, while Davy prowls about, investigating. She notes that the stories are invariably about somebody buying a dilapidated Tuscan farmhouse and renovating it with the help or hindrance of eccentric but kindly natives. The protagonists drink local wine, eat local fruit and vegetables, marvelling at their cheapness, sometimes fall in love – but almost never, she notices, with the locals – meet with disaster, overcome all their tribulations and live happily ever after.

Later in the week she will discover the other kind of book about Italy, tucked away on these same shelves: stories of bureaucracy and corruption, cautionary tales from those self-consciously in the know. She finds that she likes them even less, if anything, than the honest-to-God fantasies.

'Plenty to read,' observes Davy.

She shrugs. 'You reckon?'

She has brought her own reading matter, a bleak Scottish crime novel. She feels herself resisting the pull of the place, confused by its glamour and its outlandishness.

There is a shop down in the village with ten kinds of cheese, as many varieties of salami and pasta, tins of tomatoes and anchovies and packets of Lavazza coffee as well as shelves full of cleaning materials. There is a freezer cabinet and fresh bread, but little in the way of fruit or vegetables.

'Perhaps people grow those themselves,' says Davy.

'Perhaps they buy them in the supermarket in the next town.'

She can't seem to stop herself from making these snappy rejoinders.

Davy doesn't reply, unwilling to get into an argument. Hormones, he thinks. Hormones, she thinks too. But she feels the need to resist something. The place is too easy. She can't fathom it at all.

'*Buongiorno*,' say the locals, meeting them on the road down to the shop, smiling at the baby.

In the garden of the villa there is a fig tree, but although the figs are soft and ripe, there are holes in them where insects have bored deep inside. The rosemary is in bright blue bloom all over again. There are pots of thyme and pomegranate trees, shrub sized, with a few fruits still clinging to their branches. She is faintly disturbed by the way in which each fruit opens out, the skin stretching like a purple mouth so that the drying seeds can fall to the ground beneath.

After supper, they sit on the terrace and drink wine until the light leaches out of the sky and a thousand lamps are strung across the hills with dark valleys between. No-one lives in the valleys and the roads only dip briefly across them. They are dangerous pools of darkness between the hill-top illuminations.

'Do you know,' says Davy, who has been reading one of the cautionary tales, 'That the Italians consider it uncouth to carry on drinking wine after you've stopped eating. You can drink other things, *grappa* for instance, but not wine.'

'Not a lot of people know that,' she says.

The bed is large and comfortable and there is a cot for the baby which they place beside it. He wakes in the night for milk and she wraps him in a shawl and takes him onto the terrace so as not to wake Davy. It is still warm out there and she sits on one of the plastic chairs. The silence, above and beyond the sucking noises of the baby's lips against her breast, is absolute. The air is fresh with a faint undertone of sulphur. When she mentioned it to Davy, last night, he laughed at her.

'You and your smells! I think it's just wood smoke.'

But sitting out here, she is aware of it again, just the faintest whiff of hell. She cups the baby's head in her hand, defensively, and changes sides.

In the morning they are woken by the sound of huntsmen in the woods beyond the house.

'Christ,' says Davy. 'That's a rifle, not a shotgun.'

'What are they shooting?'

'I don't know. Birds. Rabbits. Could be wild boar I suppose.'

Later that day, they find a signboard down in the village pointing the way to a *mofetta* which seems, from the illustration, to be some kind of volcanic emission.

'I told you so.'

'What did you tell me?'

'Sulphur. I could smell it again in the night.'

About half a mile from the village they find another signpost and following a rocky track between shrubs they come across a gully where a small eruption fulminates with ash and with mud that seems to have a life of its own, bubbling and heaving in sinister fashion. There is a pool of water next to it, at what cookery books call a 'rolling boil.' The signs warn that it will be *periculoso* to go any closer because of the concentrations of CO_2 in the air.

'I wonder what the English for *mofetta* is?'

'Fumarole' she says, dredging the word up from somewhere.

'Aren't you the smart one?' says Davy.

The trees are all tagged and there is obviously some kind of scientific experiment in process. Davy wants to stay and watch the mud but she is seized with fear for the baby and heads back up the track again, not willing to wait for him. Half way up, a big brindled dog bursts from the undergrowth. She halts but it is a friendly creature, cavorting around her briefly before elbowing her aside and heading on up the track. The baby, lulled by the motion of her walking, sleeps. It has just started to rain, so when she has put some distance between herself and the fumarole, she shelters beneath the low trees to wait for Davy. The pungent scent of mint envelopes her, rising from beneath her feet As soon as she stops moving, the baby wakes up and wrinkles his nose. Perhaps he can smell the mint too or perhaps he is only hungry.

'Not now,' she whispers to him. 'You'll have to wait till we get back to the house.'

He gazes up at her with blue, unfocussed eyes and then dozes again.

She hears the snapping of twigs as somebody pushes through the undergrowth. The dog comes rushing back down the path to greet the newcomer. She is expecting to see Davy but instead, an elderly man strides out of the trees. She has an impression of a blue waterproof stretched over a bulging stomach, the gun slung over his back, pink cheeks, raindrops on grey hair. He nods to her, unsmiling, and then he is gone, the dog frisking around him. She wonders if they have ruined his day's hunting with their noise but the dog wasn't exactly subtle either.

Davy is picking his way up the track.

'Still asleep?' he asks.

'Seems to be.'

'We'll pay for it tonight,' he says, Scottish to the bone.

That was yesterday. But today they are in the Museum of Torture. They are the only visitors on this quiet afternoon, and she is gazing at an old wooden rocking horse. What is a rocking horse doing in such a place, she wonders? They have already talked about getting one for Angus. They have seen pictures in glossy magazines, sent for brochures, wondered if they will be able to afford one before their son is too big to ride it.

'It's you that wants one, really,' says Davy, and she can't deny it.

This horse is in dark wood with savage teeth and a leather saddle. Bewildered, she reads the caption.

'This rocking horse was bought by a nobleman for his son. But the six year old child became too fond of the horse and neglected his studies so that he could ride on it. The father asked a local craftsman to alter the saddle, so that riding the horse became a punishment rather than a pleasure.'

She looks more closely at the saddle and sees that somebody has fashioned it into peaks and cones of hard leather. She feels breathless, stifled, as though she can't get enough air into her lungs. She turns away, heading for the exit.

The baby, aware of her distress, stirs and wails. Outside the museum, she sways from side to side, patting his back. The rain has stopped. An old woman, perched on a stone bench in the watery sunlight, smiles up at her and indicates the seat beside her. She sits down briefly, but the bench smells of pee, so she gets up again, jiggling him, until Davy dawdles out of the museum.

'Are you alright?' he asks. 'I wondered where you'd gone.'

'I just got too hot in there. I needed some fresh air.'

'Don't think much to the horse, do you?'

'No.'

'Nasty idea. Imagine doing that.'

His composure angers her.

'Imagine,' she says.

The thought of Angus's peachy bottom in contact with those leather spikes sets her teeth on edge. Emotions clash and collide in her head. How could they? How could anybody?

They head back to the car, deciding to save the Etruscans for another day.

'You look very tired, Rosy Posy' he says, suddenly solicitous.

He only calls her Rosy Posy when he is worried about her. She thinks she might be going to cry and controls herself with an effort.

When they go back to Scotland, people will say, 'What was it like? In Tuscany? Was it nice?'

'It wasn't what I expected.'

'What did you expect?'

'I think I sort of expected the Cotswolds with sunshine. All those Sunday supplements. You know?'

'And?'

'And it's nothing like that. It's much more savage. A much more savage place altogether.'

'Didn't you like it then?' her friends and relatives will say, disappointed.

'I loved it. It just wasn't what I expected. That's all.'

After the museum, they drive back to the house and later on they walk down into the village for provisions. The houses there are dilapidated but orderly. She is lost in thoughts about the lives of these people, enmeshed in her own curiosity. She wants to open each neat front door and peer in. She tries to read the inhabitants from their possessions. She even finds herself examining the washing, strung out on lines from window to window and across terraces: trousers, underwear, towels, a pillowcase with a print of a cat's face, a Mickey Mouse duvet cover.

When she sees an elderly woman buying pasta, cheese, pancetta and eggs, she imagines the meal, pictures a family eating together around a big table. Her own grandmother is dead; her parents separated and remarried other people long ago. Davy isn't close to his family either. She has a fleeting vision of herself running after this woman.

Take me with you, she thinks. Let me come home with you. Let me sit in your kitchen while you cook. Let me tell you what has happened to me. Comfort me with food. Feed me on pasta. Fill me with potatoes roasted with olive oil and rosemary. Bake me a chestnut cake and panna cotta with speckles of vanilla. Creamy panna cotta that slides down like mother's milk. Let me live in a book about your life, where I might feel safe.

The woman stretches out a wrinkled hand and pats the baby's head. '*Bellissimo!*' she says.

That night, the baby refuses to sleep. Colicky, he struggles, girns and moans, pulling his dimpled knees close to his chest. He wants to suckle but her milk does nothing to comfort him. At last he falls asleep, sprawled on Davy's chest. Then they tuck him down between them in the bed. Her mother and her health visitor would frown at this, but she doesn't care. Some nights it is the only way they can get any rest. He is a big boy and though he always rolls onto his tummy in his cot, he invariably sleeps safely on his back when he is in bed with them, his breathing peacefully tuned to theirs. Even in sleep they are aware of his presence. He lies between them like a small oven, radiating warmth.

'I love the feel of him there,' says Davy, unexpectedly. 'Don't you, Ros?'

The latest childcare fad is something called 'controlled crying.'

'Mothers who learn to let their babies cry themselves to sleep have better nights and less postnatal depression,' said one report, pointed out to her by her GP. She irritated him by telling him that this seemed so unscientific as to be meaningless. Maybe mothers who learn to let their babies cry are unfeeling. Maybe they don't have postnatal depression at all. And what exactly do the researchers mean by 'better nights' since breast fed babies generally wake up for a feed or sometimes two? The doctor couldn't answer any of these questions and retreated into disgruntled silence.

'That's my Ros,' said Davy when she told him about it afterwards.

But one of Davy's colleagues at work is following the regime to the letter.

'It works,' he told Davy. 'My wife wasn't convinced at first, but I persuaded her, and it works. You should try it.'

'God's sake,' said Davy. 'They prosecute people for doing that.'

'For controlled crying?'

'For making young primates sleep alone in small cages. They call it animal cruelty.'

Davy can never hold his tongue either. It's one more thing they have in common.

Now they lie in bed, in a villa in Tuscany, the three of them in a row.

She thinks 'Roll over, roll over, so they all rolled over and one fell out.'

Terror assails her. 'What would he do without me?' she thinks. 'What would they do, both of them, if anything happened to me?'

Davy stirs, aware of her unease.

'Are you alright?'

'Yes. Just a bit panicky.'

'Slow your breathing.'

'I'm trying.'

She turns over and watches the baby in the half light from the hallway. Expressions flit across his face, experimental emotions, as though he is auditioning for the man he will become.

'Nobody told me,' she says quietly.

'They told us it would change our lives. Everyone said that and we didn't believe them.'

'But they never told me it would hurt this much.'

All the ante-natal care had been about choices. Birth plans. Breast is best. Not once had anyone mentioned this pain.

Davy grimaces. 'I seem to remember one friend of yours talking about shitting a melon.'

'I don't mean that.'

'You told me you'd forgotten about the pain as soon as he was born.'

'So I have.'

'Well I can't forget it. Seeing you like that. I thought I might lose you.'

'But nobody told us about this pain, did they?'

'What?' he says, really alarmed now. 'What pain?'

'Don't you feel it? Or is it only me? It can't only be me. I keep thinking of that bloody rocking horse.'

'I know. It was horrible.'

'It's as though I've lost some shield, some protective coating. I'm a hostage to my own imagination and it hurts!'

There are paedophiles, terrorists, wars, earthquakes, tsunamis. Sometimes the news seems to be about nothing but distressed or dying children. Despair overwhelms her several times a day. Even films and other fictions are unbearably poignant.

'Oh God!' she says. 'What will happen to him if I'm not here?'

'You're not going anywhere, are you?'

'No.'

'Well then.'

'But don't you see?' she tells him. 'It isn't just him.' She hesitates. 'It's every child. It's like being mother to the whole world.'

He lies there for a moment, looking at the ceiling. 'I know,' he says, unexpectedly. Just for a moment, she sees his face crumble into vulnerability. 'I do know. Father too. Father to the whole world as well.'

He props himself up on one elbow and kisses his son's cheek.

'This is a kit of first aid when necessary,' he says. 'Isn't it Angus?'

The baby stirs and flexes his perfect fingers.

From outside comes the first crackle and echo of gunfire. The morning slaughter has begun.

The Butterfly Bowl

The bowl was beautiful in its simplicity. Debbie's great great grandfather, Charles Ogilvy, had brought it back with him from China, where he had been a missionary until failing health forced him to come home to Scotland. With him had come his collection of Oriental curios: pottery, densely embroidered silk hangings, as neat on the back as on the front, bronzes, painted masks, carved ivory fans. For six months, he was very ill indeed. But Isobel, his Scottish nurse, pulled him through the worst and then married him. She was a farmer's daughter, a big, blossoming, square-jawed woman, a picture of health and strength. Death himself probably quailed before her vitality. There was a sepia wedding picture of the couple, Isobel smiling fiercely in white satin, with a vast bouquet of lilies and roses, Charles in a too-big suit, staring calmly at the camera from behind a luxuriant moustache.

Charles had survived to become minister of a small country church and Isobel bore him four children. She outlived him of course. In fact she lived long enough to know her great grand-child, Debbie's mother, and died at the age of ninety three. Debbie's mother only just remembered her and even then could never be quite sure whether it was a genuine memory or something created by her imagination, some compound of family tales and the few surviving photographs. She was remembered as a formidable woman whose brusque manner had disguised her essential kindness. But there was one thing for which the family could never quite forgive her.

'She threw out great grandfather's Chinese collection,' said Debbie's mother. 'Just got rid of it, bit by bit. She had no idea of the value of it. She hated it.'

It seemed incomprehensible to Debbie, in this age of TV shows, all aimed at persuading people that there might be something of value lurking in every attic. But the truth was that Isobel had found the collection sinister and foreign and quite unsuitable for furnishing a country manse. 'Heathen rubbish,' she had called it. She loathed every piece of it except one and gradually disposed of it. She gave away the bigger statues and bronzes to her husband's colleagues, or donated them to parish jumble sales and the annual manse garden party. The more obviously pagan things were simply put out with the rubbish. Isobel's dustbins became something of a legend in the district. Charles however, put his foot down about the little china bowl.

'I don't care what you throw out, my dear. But not that bowl. It was given to me by a very dear friend.'

'Some *Chinaman* I'll be bound' she said scornfully, but Charles was not to be defeated and his sudden passion disconcerted her.

'Whatever nationality my friend was, this bowl is very precious to me. If you throw it out I'll never forgive you, Issie. I won't have it. Do you hear?'

Isobel agreed. She could afford to be magnanimous. Besides, she was fond of the bowl. It was the only thing in the entire collection that she was comfortable with. Like Isobel herself, it was simple and straightforward: no pretensions, no fuss.

It was many years before Charles could bring himself to tell her that the bowl was not quite so simple or straightforward as she supposed. He wondered why she hadn't stumbled upon its secret by accident, but he could only imagine that when she washed the bowl, her water was soapy, and she wasn't a very observant woman. Much to his surprise, when he eventually explained it to her, it only served to endear the bowl to her still more. Charles had some vague idea that she might be able to sell it after he died but, quite uncharacteristically for someone so practical, she refused. Instead she gave the bowl to her eldest daughter who passed it down through the family. And when Debbie was ten, her mother told her its secret.

Debbie remembered the day vividly for its combination of tragedy and magic. Her cat had been killed. She had been playing with it in the garden – it was little more than a kitten – and suddenly it had darted through the wrought iron bars of the gate, right into the path of a car. Debbie was inconsolable, although they had a proper funeral and buried the little mangled body in a shoe box under the Japanese Cherry. And so, worn down by the crying and the recriminations, her mother had eventually brought out the bowl and said, 'Look. Let me show you something special.'

'It's only an old bowl!'

'No. It's a bit more than that, darling. Watch. I'll fill it with water.'

There she was, sobbing one minute and the next, utterly silent, for the water in the bowl was full of butterflies. Some skill, long since lost, had allowed the images to be imprisoned in a clear glaze so that when there was water in the bowl, butterflies were reflected there. A finger dipped casually in the water made them dance, made them move as the water moved, break apart and reform themselves. The butterflies were, thought Debbie, like little shimmering rainbow ghosts, trapped and fluttering there.

She had kept the bowl for years and kept its secret too. She had cared for it and washed it and looked at the butterflies only occasionally. She almost came to take it for granted. But then she would fill it with water again and, seeing the miracle of it renewed, would find herself wondering about the person who had given it to her great great grandfather. Whoever it was must have been very fond of him, she thought, or very indebted to him for some service. But perhaps it had been given to him by a woman. A woman in love? What else could demand the sacrifice of such a treasure?

Then, at the age of twenty seven, Debbie herself fell in love. There had been men in her life before, but none like this. Tom was a fellow lecturer at the college where Debbie worked. He was some twelve years older, taught drama and considered himself to be more of a practitioner than a teacher. He didn't really want to be a teacher at all, unlike Debbie who enjoyed her work, teaching English to mature students and young people for whom school had been a trial. She liked her students, liked the fact that they were volunteers rather than conscripts, liked the way in which she could convey something of her love for the written word, even if her priority had to be getting them through their exams.

She was new to the college but she had noticed Tom on her first day. It was hard not to notice him. He was a produced play-wright, which made him seem like a very big fish in their small town pond. He was tall and slender and, if not exactly handsome, then she thought that he had the right sort of face. All its planes and angles pleased her. People liked him. They listened when he spoke. He made them laugh although there was always an edge of sarcasm in his voice. He invariably seemed to be at the centre of a cheerful, admiring group. Debbie was much too shy to intrude.

One evening, she found herself walking behind him in the cor-ridor. She had been teaching an English class while he was doing a scriptwriting course in the room next door. He was being borne off to the pub by a crowd of his students, mostly female, and as they swept past, he whirled around suddenly and called her name.

'Debbie?' he said. 'Debbie isn't it?' And it sounded extra-ordinarily sweet to her to hear him saying her name. 'So you're taking the dreaded evening classes as well?'

She smiled and nodded.

'Go on,' he said to his students. 'I'll catch you up.'

She was putting on her coat. He held it for her. She was intensely aware of him, his physical presence. She could smell his breath, sweet on her face, the slight scent of peppermint as she turned towards him.

'Come and have a drink with us. You probably need it as much as I do!'

So she went with them to a nearby pub. All his smiles were directed at her with a curious intimacy as though he had known her for a long time. All his jokes included her. He had a knack of making her feel as if she were on his side, and she was captivated by him.

It came to her later, as these things do, that what most endeared him to her was what he had in common with so many men. With her, he was able to drop the bright shield of his confidence and seem vulnerable. He had to teach, he told her, so that he could get the money to write, to work on his plays, because there was no money in theatre. But when he taught, he couldn't write properly. He needed time, time to think. Besides, theatre was a world where networking was vital. Not only did you have to write, but you had to show face, spend time in theatre bars, chat to people at press nights, be available.

After that first evening in the pub there were others: trips to the cinema and the theatre – although he was an uneasy companion in the theatre, over-critical and given to sighing and fidgeting – meals in small restaurants, kisses and caresses afterwards. She had not yet slept with him. She was nervous, unsure of him at the back of her mind. Perhaps she had an inkling of some enormous self-preoccupation that lay in his heart and left only a small amount of space for her. But she thought about him all the time, even in class when she was reading set books with the students and discussing the character of this or that protagonist.

In his spare time, Tom was working on one of his own scripts with a group of his students. They were rehearsing in the upstairs room of a pub and he asked Debbie to come along. It was late autumn, a chilly evening with the smell of smoke in the air. She took time over her hair and spent ages on her makeup. The room was stuffy and the sound of hilarity drifted up the stairs from the bar below. Tom's play was a grimly violent coming-of-age drama about a group of deprived young men. There were no female characters at all. Debbie took the script and acted as prompt, but she thought that the students were all rather good, better than Tom's play, which seemed to her to be pretentious and over-written. Loyally, she quelled those feelings. After all, what did she know about it? Quite a lot, really, said the rational part of her mind, the part that was not blinded by desire.

Afterwards, as they waited for a cab, he seemed morose and dissatisfied. 'They're not professionals and it shows,' he grumbled.

'Well I think it's excellent!' She slipped her hand through his arm, feeling the solid warmth of him beneath her fingers.

'I do love you!' he said, looking down at her, and that seemed a kind of milestone, because he had never said it before. So now it was alright to tell him that she loved him. That was the rule. You never said 'I love you' to a man first. But once he had said it to you, you could say it back again. She didn't really believe that, had read it in a magazine years ago when she was in her early teens, ten things never to say to your man. But for some reason, it had stuck. Even now.

'Do you want to come in?' she said, when the cab stopped outside her flat.

'I love you, I love you,' she told him in bed that night.

When she woke in the morning, warm and sated, with his

arm thrown across her, she had no regrets at all. She extricated herself, made coffee and croissants, brought a tray back through and watched him sleeping for a while.

He was divorced. His wife had remarried and moved to London. There had been no children and it had been as amicable a parting as such things ever are. He still saw her from time to time. Nobody could stay angry with him for long. But he supposed he wasn't easy to live with. Writers and actors never were.

'The sliver of ice in the heart and all that,' he said with a little grin. Maybe actors were even worse. Marry an actor and you never knew who you were living with from one day to the next. His ex-wife was an actor, so he knew all about that.

Now, whenever he said, 'I love you,' she was supposed to say, 'I love you too.' If she didn't, he would say, 'Don't you love me? Tell me you love me.'

'You must know that I do!'

'Ah,' he said with a smile, with a wide, wide smile that was almost a groan, 'But I need constant reassurance.'

It was true. He needed somebody to be forever telling him that he was loved. She was helpless in the face of such need. Yes, she told him, he was a great writer. A fine playwright. But even if he wasn't a great writer she would still love him.

Part of this, the part about love, was true. But part of it was a lie. She didn't think he was a great writer. She thought he might be good, but not really great. She couldn't believe that the way he wrote, which seemed coldly misogynistic, might be the truth about him. Instead she blamed herself, trying desperately to think of something new and profound to say. It didn't matter. He didn't want her to say profound things. He just wanted her to say that she loved him and his work too, and keep on saying it.

Time passed, the year turned, and they fell into a kind of routine, spending their weekends together, seeing each other at work as well. Sometimes they would socialise with other people but he was impatient with her friends and gradually, Debbie found herself drawn into his theatrical circle, hardly ever seeing the women friends with whom she had once spent most of her free time. She would have said that she was supremely happy. But he exhausted her. You were supposed to be able to keep on giving love as though it came from some magical well-spring, but it wasn't really like that. Not in this case. The more you gave, the more tired you became. The more tired you became, the more you were inclined to give. Soon there would be nothing left of her at all.

One night, Tom had been more miserable than usual, full of anxiety about his work, and Debbie was desperate to help him. In this frame of mind, with all her resources of love and sympathy drained from her, she took down the china bowl and filled it full of water.

'Nice old bowl,' said Tom. 'Nice glaze.'

'It's nicer than you think!'

She set it down on the table. It was spring and the evening light fell on the bowl. The window was open and the perfume of lilac drifted in. For a long time afterwards, the scent of lilac would give her a sad, sinking feeling like a premonition of disaster.

'My God!' he said. 'Butterflies! This is weird.' He laughed. 'Really weird. Some gimmick. How does it work?'

She felt inexplicably tearful. And then she felt impelled to make some sort of gesture. Or perhaps it was only the fatigue speaking. Everything was given to Tom, so why not this?

'It's yours if you want it.'

Looking back later, she realised that what she had meant was, 'It's ours. Together. Our bowl.'

He picked it up and the butterflies danced as the water moved.

It made her feel dizzy to see it held so firmly in his strong hands. She had a frisson of desire and apprehension.

'It must be very old.'

'Very.'

'And it must be worth a bloody fortune,' he added, setting it down on the table. 'How much do you pay out in insurance?'

'Insurance?'

He stared at her in amazement. 'You don't mean to tell me that this isn't even insured?'

'It's never been insured.'

'But what if it was stolen or broken?'

'Who would know? Who would know to steal it? It's just a plain white china bowl.'

He shrugged. 'Word gets about.'

'But nobody knows.' She had expected him to understand at once and now she was having to explain everything. 'Nobody's ever known. Only me and my mother. And now you. And you'll keep the secret. Won't you?'

She looked at him as he sat poring over the bowl and caught an expression that was something between wonderment and avarice flitting across his face.

'Deb, will you lend it to me?'

'I told you. You can have it.'

But she hadn't expected him to take it. Not really.

He shook his head. 'Just lend it to me for a week or so. I'll take good care of it. I promise.'

He would say no more than that. She wrapped it up carefully, and he took it away with him. But that night, when she looked at the spot on the shelf where it had stood for so many years, she felt bereaved. The strength of her feeling for the bowl surprised her. She fretted and worried about it, while Tom was mysterious and gleeful. But he would not tell her what he had done with it.

'It'll be back,' was all he would say.

When he did bring it back, about a week later, he brought a bottle of champagne too, opened it and poured a couple of glasses. Relief at seeing the bowl made her foolishly generous.

'You could have kept it, you know,' she lied. 'I didn't really want it back.'

'I took it through to Edinburgh.'

'Why? Why would you do that?'

'I took it to one of the big auction houses. Don't you want to know what it's worth?'

For years, the thought that she was hoarding something very precious had lurked at the back of her mind. For years, the thought had just occasionally surfaced that the bowl ought to be in a museum. But then she imagined it in a glass case, surrounded by burglar alarms. Worse, stored away where nobody could see it. They probably wouldn't even fill it with water. Certainly nobody would be able to touch it. Nobody would ever be allowed to bend too close to the fluttering shadows. To all intents and purposes it would be dead.

'No, Tom,' she said. 'Don't tell me.'

Tom didn't seem to hear her. 'They could hardly believe it. In fact it caused something of a sensation. They had to call in other experts. More expert experts. Debbie, it's worth thousands. The Chinese are buying back all their antiques. Maybe hundreds of thousands. Just think what we can do with the money.'

What was he saying? What money?

'A small fortune. Christ, a large one. Oh Deb, it's a dream come true. I can write every day. Set up my own theatre company if I want. You can help. We can really make it work. It'll be wonderful.'

He stopped, aware of her silence.

'What's the matter?' he asked.

'I don't want to know how much it's worth.'

It was his turn to be bemused.

'But it's much too valuable to keep, Debbie. It would be like a millstone around our necks.'

She picked it up. 'It's just a china bowl.'

He hovered close to her, his hands stretching out, involuntarily.

'Put it down for God's sake. You might drop it.'

'I've never dropped it yet!'

She set it down again, but he was already moving away from her, pacing up and down, working himself into a rage.

'I don't understand you!' He whirled around on her. 'Do you want to teach English all your life?'

'I wouldn't mind. I don't really want to help you run a theatre group, Tom.'

'Oh that was just a possibility.' He moved impatiently towards her, took her by the shoulders. 'You could do anything you wanted. Where's your ambition?'

She felt the familiar physical sensations at his closeness. And he must have seen it in her eyes, because he pulled her closer still.

'You're having me on, Debbie, aren't you?' His voice was suddenly gentle, loving. 'You don't mean this. Not when it's worth all this. Hundreds of thousands, they said. Collectors bidding for it online. People from all over the world. Nobody could resist that. And the publicity. My God, think of the publicity!'

'What do you mean?'

'Newspapers. Television. Think how good it would be for my career.'

She ducked out of his embrace. His mouth twisted in an ugly little grimace. 'I thought you loved me!'

'I meant for us to share it.'

'And I want to do what's best for us. I want to sell it for us. For you and me. So that we can be happy together. I've told them we will. I've signed a form.'

'Well you can unsign it. You can tell them you made a mistake. It wasn't yours to sell.'

She should never have shown him the bowl. 'Listen,' she said, trying to take his hands, willing him to see it her way. 'It's too precious to sell. I love it. There's magic in it.'

He thrust her away. 'It's a gimmick. It's only priceless because we don't know how they did it. But it's just a knack all the same. Just a question of technique. The person who made this was a craftsman. There's magic in real creativity. Like mine. But not in this. The guy that made this – he probably made all the money he could out of it. They were probably ten a penny at one time.'

She said nothing. There was nothing to say.

'Don't I matter to you?' he said at last, with that whining, faintly threatening edge to his voice. She had heard it before and it frightened her. The sheer magnetism of him frightened her. He was used to getting his own way.

'Of course you do.'

'Well, you gave the bowl to me. It's mine now. I can sell it if I want to.'

He was behaving like a selfish little boy, perhaps hoping that she would play mother to the child in him for one more time.

'But I don't want to sell it.'

'I've told a newspaper. I phoned them. I said we'd be selling it. They're sending a photographer round. The happy couple with their new found treasure.'

'Then you can tell him to go away again, can't you?'

He picked the bowl up.

'What are you doing?'

'I'm going to put it in the bank. I'm going to put it in the bank until the sale.'

He was so much bigger, so much stronger. If he wanted to take it, how could she ever stop him? But how could she ever let the bowl go?

She made a swift lunge at it before it disappeared inside Tom's bag.

They were like children, squabbling over a toy. At exactly the same moment, both of them let go of the bowl and it fell to the floor with a clatter.

'Oh my God!' he said. Then he was down on his knees. He picked it up. Inside, a jagged crack arced across the white surface.

'It'll be alright!' But he shook his head, even as he said it. 'Surely it'll be alright, Debbie. Won't it?'

She took the bowl from him but she couldn't bear to look at him.

'Get out!' she said.

He went without another word.

She put the bowl back on the shelf. Her fingers were trembling, so she poured herself another glass of champagne. The sun had set. She felt cold and switched on the lamp and the electric fire. She wondered whether to cry but there seemed no point in tears.

The doorbell rang. She thought it might be a contrite Tom, but it was a young man with fair hair and a pink face and a camera slung over one shoulder. It was pulling his baggy, hand knitted sweater all askew. 'I believe you have a Chinese bowl,' he said. 'Your fiancé phoned.'

She asked him in and offered him the last of the wine. He seemed surprised but accepted readily enough.

'I don't have a fiancé,' she said, stretching her aching face into a grin. 'I have some friends who are into practical jokes. I expect that's what it was. I'm sorry to disappoint you.'

'The man on the phone said it was a plain white china bowl. When you filled it with water you could see butterflies in it. Some strange property of the glaze.'

'And you believed that?'

'No – well – yes. We wondered.'

'A bit far fetched, don't you think?'

'Perhaps.'

'Sounds like a legend to me. You have been taken in, haven't you?'

'And you don't have any bowl at all?'

'Oh yes. My great great grandfather brought all kinds of things back from China. He was a missionary there. But it's just a white bowl. Nothing special about it. I should know. I've washed it often enough. I keep it for sentimental reasons. That's all.'

She took him over to the shelf and showed him the bowl.

'Broken at one time?' he said.

She nodded. 'Yes.'

'You can see, can't you? There.' He gestured at the fine crack. She winced.

He finished his champagne.

'Well, I'd better be going.' He stood up. 'Sorry to trouble you. It was a nice idea. And thanks for the bubbly.'

'A very nice idea. But I don't believe such things exist. Do you?' she said at the door.

He turned back to her. 'I like to think they might have, at one time.' He smiled at her. 'Would you sell such a bowl if you had one?'

'I might. You never know what you might do if the price is high enough.'

She closed the door after him and brought a jug of water from the kitchen. Slowly she poured it into the bowl. It didn't leak, that was something. Her heart was thumping. She could feel the beat of it in her throat. She didn't look into the bowl immediately but carried it across the room to where the light was brighter. She placed it on the table and stared into it.

She saw water gleaming in the lamplight. Nothing else.

She sat for a long time, staring into the bowl. Willing the butterflies to appear. Presently she took it back into the kitchen, emptied it, dried it and then put it back on the shelf. From here it looked no different. You might almost imagine that it was exactly the same.

But as time went by, she began to wonder if they had ever existed at all, those ghost butterflies: a bowl full of dancing butterflies to captivate a wife, to comfort a grieving child, a gift for a lover. She could remember, but the memory had no substance. Whoever had created the bowl was long dead. She could not ask him what he had meant by it. She could not ask him if he had cared as much about his creation as she came to, so many years later, or if he simply saw it as a good commercial proposition. The uncertainty blighted her remembrance of its beauty. She remembered the butterflies and how she felt about them in the same way that she remembered that she had once loved Tom, deeply, passionately. Neither feeling had any substance now. But she would always be glad of the bowl. Glad of it sitting there upon her shelf. Glad, even if no matter how she poured and poured the clear water, she would never see butterflies in it again.

The Man In The Moon

Two young men are cleaning Tadolini's Eve in the Kibble Palace on this hot May morning. A thousand hands have grimed her flesh, but she remains cool as a linen sheet. They dab her leg with cotton wool, unaware of the blood and bone beneath the stone. 'Folk stroke her,' one says, and indeed there are black smears along the skin. Eve wears a chaste garland of leaves draped around her hips, while outside, the blousy tulips riot. Boys and girls embrace on the grass. Spring's momentum pushes the year on. And an old woman sits, rueful in the sun, sad to be alone among such abundance.

She closes her eyes, considering the nature of friendship. Considering the nature of love. A few months ago, she met him again by chance, an old lover. Today, briefly, she indulges in the memory of their first meeting, walking down these same city streets at dusk, when shopping crowds had left, when music spilled from doors, when candles on restaurant tables were lit, when crisp linen was folded and glasses gleamed, inviting the communion of food from lip to lip. She remembers how a sudden shower slaked the dust. She sees again the audacious city in the rain and all the street smelled sweet, as though some ancient garden were lurking behind those walls. Pigeons picked about the paving stones and the light leached slowly out of the sky while stone angels danced among the heights. And hand found hand. And anything was possible because she was young.

She opens her eyes, forcing these visions to flee, banished by sunlight. That was then. This is all too stubbornly now. But in the Kibble Palace on this hot May morning, she also finds the memory of their instant familiarity as though time were running backwards from now to then. Also the way he sat and stood and his habit of touching her arm and his frown. More than that, there were conversations about books, poetry, music. She remembers fat letters waiting in her hallway and phone calls which neither of them could end. There was tenderness and the promise of a future. But it was a too-sudden love that could not possibly last. It did not last.

Besides, he lied as the birds sing.

Their time together was ridiculously short. All too soon, she became unsure of him. There were a million uncertainties. She remembers journeys when they tried to reach some resolution but were clean out of resolve, with both of them behaving badly and neither of them loving very well. Now she cannot understand why he loomed so large in her life, nor why his betrayal seemed so momentous, nor why he led her on to let her fall so carelessly. Drifting to the ground like discarded paper.

She remembers the litany of all this. She remembers the first time they kissed but not the last. She remembers angrily turning him from her door, but not what she said. Why seek to apportion blame? She has been very happy since. When he left he took some of the words from her mouth. Recently, as they rediscovered a tentative acquaintance, she thought he had returned them to her in a plain wrapper and she was briefly grateful. But now she sees that she was wrong. The words themselves were facile. The words they shared were nothing.

The truth was that he was always miserly with his time, even in friendship, hoarding his minutes as though he couldn't bear to waste a single one on trivialities. Did he really see or understand the first thing about her? She doubts it now. Nor did she know the first thing about him. The older she grows the less she knows what goes on in anybody's head. The inexperienced young flirt with catastrophe, while sad old souls walk tightropes, appreciate happy endings without believing in them, all too aware of the instability of things. We are frail, insubstantial as smoke on water, ghost whispers. We are chaos and confusion. We build our houses along the edges of volcanoes. We wander unawares through mine-fields, court hurricanes and disaster. Nothing holds. Everything is breakable. But love is where you find it. Real love can be mended. Real love lies in the spaces between.

This was never love. Not really. Not once.

She considers Woodlands Road in autumn. Men are wheeling melons heaped in barrows. She is on her way to an art history class. A girl pushes her child in a pram, the wheels swishing over the damp pavement, crushing the leaves that have drifted from the trees in Kelvingrove Park. The girl wears a saffron sari like the sun. The child laughs up at his mother. They are engrossed in each other. For this small spell, nothing will shift or shake them. They are a shining certainty. Young men loiter outside shops, or unload vans, or converse in staccato tones. A dog trots down the street, heading for the ragged park, absorbed in a world of scent. Each to his own. But summer seems infinitely distant now. And that's because it is.

Sometimes she stops in a cafe, sitting alone with hands cupped around a latte, warming her wintry fingers and her heart with the comfort of coffee. The other members of the class are even older, make her feel younger than she really is, complimenting her on her bright clothes, treating her like the younger woman she so obviously is not, polishing each transient pleasure until it gleams. The lecturer shows slides of Breughel, Rembrandt, Goya, a measured canter through the history of the visual image. He's a frail old man with a lifetime's experience and every week, he says something to open their eyes, to make them see. The room's a cocoon: warm, dark, inducing a kind of trance across which these splendid images of lovers, mothers and babies, and angels flit, the words a soothing counterpoint to her dreams. She walks back again from week to week, watching the city sink slowly into winter, thinking about rites of passage, thinking about these visions of experience and what they mean.

One late afternoon in Woodlands Road, near dark, she sees a lamp in a high window, a pale imprisoned face, its features as vaguely human as the moon. And she knows with certainty that the man at the back of her mind is an idea merely, a false conceit, by no means what she once thought him. He's an under drawing. More than that, a hidden image. Not even a very good one. She sees that she cannot now and never will fathom him. Nor does she want to. She yawns with the boredom of it. Love's seldom where we think we'll find it. Nor is it conditional. This was not love; it was not even friendship. He always was other and elsewhere. She sees that she was attempting to impose a human face, a warm image on something as remote, as impenetrably aloof, as cold and old as the man in the moon, for whom this exile was once foolishly, just a little homesick.

Now, in the Kibble Palace on this hot May morning, they are cleaning Tadolini's Eve. She closes her eyes, considering the nature of love, considering the nature of friendship. So many years. How on that chance encounter, they slid back into apparent familiarity, like seals into water. But it was a brief mirage. A public display. There is no going back. They are changed irrevocably, and nobody can reclaim the past. Nor should they even try.

She sees that the fault lies entirely with herself for dwelling on lost gardens. Our old loves slide away from us like cotton wool along a marble arm. Significant then. Meaningless now. Passion wanes. Only genuine affection survives and this was never affection. It was something else, something other and alien. The lads are texting, all work forgotten in the urge to make contact and why not, at such a time of their lives, on such a day? Eve gazes to her right, distressed. They touch her, but do not see her. Unwatched, she ceases to exist as all old women do. She's looking for Adam under the sun, but the apple was sour, the serpent an excuse. What matters is this and only this. A toddler stares, full of the day's joy among the tulips, flinging his little hat in the air, baring his head to the sun.

Stained Glass

The renovation had taken time, effort and money but now it was almost complete. Jack had bought the stone cottage in the long village street because he wanted somewhere of his own, a place on which he could lavish a little affection. The house had originally been part of a terrace. On the right it was still attached to the row of old weavers' houses but on the left there was a gap where another cottage had long ago been demolished. The space was randomly paved with small, square tiles, the remains of the cottage's Victorian or Georgian floor perhaps, with long grass and weeds sprouting between them.

'Room for possible extension,' the estate agent's schedule had said.

Jack had also acquired the demolished cottage's wilderness of a garden as part of his own, though as yet he had hardly done any gardening. He had been much too busy on the house. His neighbour on the right hand side was an elderly widow who lived alone. A friendly pub was within walking distance and for the first time since the sudden death of his wife, a couple of years earlier, he found himself achieving a kind of contentment. He had worked steadily on the house throughout the winter and now, with the coming of spring, he could look with pleasure on newly sanded and waxed floors, a restored stone fireplace, a white tiled bathroom and an oak kitchen. He had resisted the temptation to buy an Aga. That had been his wife's dream, not his, and besides, funds were getting low.

Like all old houses, the cottage had objected to the disturbance, throwing a hundred problems at him. But there had been a certain satisfaction in finding solutions. In his more imaginative moments, he thought that he and the house had sized each other up and grown used to each other. All its nightly noises – alarming at first – were familiar now: the creak and rustle of cooling wood, the tap, tap of hot water in the pipes, the occasional mousy scuttering from the loft. He had set a few traps but caught only field mice and the odd shrew. He had felt so sorry for them that he had bought an electronic device to deter them and, to his relief, it seemed to be working. There were idiosyncrasies too: the spare bedroom door that wouldn't stay shut, but swung open without warning, the draughty spot at the bend in the stairs, the faint whiff of pipe tobacco, although Jack had never smoked. None of these things worried him, although his occasional visitors – friends from the city – commented on them. But there was a consistency about them that was reassuring. Now he could begin to think about getting the garden into shape. He anticipated the work involved with real pleasure.

He was a young man and had taken the loss of his wife very badly. They had planned children, but later. Now, he was torn between sorrow over what might have been and relief that he hadn't been left alone to cope with a family. Unable to bear the pain of so many associations in the city where they had been together since graduation, he had asked for a transfer and come to work in a nearby town where there was a smaller, quieter branch of his company. He didn't care so much for promotion any more. All his hopes for the future had been shared with his wife. Now she was gone, he was content to spend all his free time on the house.

'He hasn't an idle bone in his body,' they said of him in the village and that was praise indeed, for they were slow to accept strangers. But they had begun to like him.

The house, however, lacked one finishing touch and at first he was at a loss how to remedy it. At the bend in the stairs, quite high up, at the back of the cottage, there was a round stained glass window, like a small porthole. Or rather there had once been such a window but what was left of it was so cracked and splintered that he had had to seal it with hardboard to keep out the winter draughts until he should decide what to do about it. He was very much afraid that he was going to have to fill the space with clear glass but, for some reason, the idea disappointed him. He was conscientious about such things, liking the unusual features that characterised the place.

Jack had been discussing the problem one night in the pub with a friend who had come down from the city to admire the work on the cottage. Billy, the landlord, happened to overhear their conversation, or it may have been that he was eavesdropping. At any rate, later on in the evening, he approached Jack.

'About that stained glass ...'

'Yes?'

'I could let you have a window. I didn't know yours was broken. This one's just the same.'

Jack was mystified. 'You could?'

'Aye. It came from the cottage next door to yours, just before it was demolished. That was before my time, but they took out the glass. So my father said. I suppose someone thought it was too nice to throw away. It's been up in our loft for years. You're welcome to it if you can use it.'

'Why was the other cottage demolished?' asked Jack's friend.

'I wouldn't know.' Billy shrugged. 'It lay empty for years. Eventually the dry rot and the wet rot and the woodworm got to it. The way it nearly got to yours, Jack.' He mopped at the bar with a cloth. 'They were always a pair those two houses. Built at the same time, I suppose. But it was empty for a long time and houses in this village weren't fetching the prices they are today. Eventually, nobody could be bothered with it. Not then, anyway. And it was well before the old cottages were listed, so it was condemned and demolished.'

'Shame,' said Jack's friend.

'Yes, but it's given me a nice bit of extra land,' said Jack. 'I'm going to have my vegetable garden there.'

'You're really into all this self sufficiency stuff, aren't you?' asked his friend, draining his glass.

'Not really. But I've always wanted to grow veggies.'

'Tatties,' said Billy.

'What?'

'Potatoes, that's what you have to grow in the first year. Cleans the ground. You'll need seed potatoes.'

'Will I?'

'You will. I can give you some. And since you've got the land, you may as well have the window.'

Billy brought it round the next day. It was wrapped neatly in yellowing newspaper. Jack took it out and set it carefully on the floor, side-tracked for a moment by the old advertisements for corsetry and tricycles. He folded the newspaper carefully. Worth keeping, he thought. He could see that the window was a fine piece of work. The glass was clear red with an intricate little chain of flowers and leaves as a border. Afraid of damaging it, he contracted a local glazier to set it in and was pleased to notice how the afternoon sun cast a rosy glow through the red glass, shedding a beam of light over his stairs.

The window fascinated him.

Every time he passed through his hallway, he found himself pausing to admire it. The morning after its installation, a fine spring Sunday, he took a bowl of warm water up to his landing, stood on a stepladder and began to clean the old glass, carefully sponging away the traces of putty left by the glazier. Presently, however, he found his attention focussed on the patch of garden he could see outside. The stone walls of his house were very thick and they blinkered his view. Also, the glass itself had a flaw in it that slightly blurred his vision but leaning a little to the left of his window, he found that he was looking at what seemed to be a cherry tree. He could just make out blossom as well as a patch of grass with scattered petals beneath. Somebody was sitting there. The warp in the glass prevented him from seeing clearly, but it seemed to be a young woman dressed in light clothing, her head bent over her lap. She might be reading or even sewing. He screwed up his eyes. It occurred to him that he must be looking into next door's garden: the one to the right of his own house. The window must have somehow funnelled his vision.

The old lady must have visitors; a grand-daughter perhaps. There was a suggestion of long dark hair, a slim frame beneath. He stopped in his work of cleaning, his hand poised over the glass. A young man had come up and slipped his arms around the girl from behind. Jack saw a pale shirt, pink in the light from the glass, though he guessed it must be white. A loose shirt, dark trousers. The girl reached up her hands to grasp his. The man bent over and kissed the top of her head. Then she half rose, and they were in each other's arms, embracing passionately in the sunlight.

Jack was embarrassed. He felt himself beginning to blush. It was as though he had intruded on their sudden moment of intimacy, although they couldn't possibly know it, wouldn't – surely – be able to see him. He took himself downstairs so that he shouldn't be tempted to spy on the couple from the bedroom window. He was a good-natured young man and felt as though it wasn't quite honest to watch them like this.

But the stained glass held its own attraction. The morning wore on towards lunch time. Whenever he had reason to pass through the hall, going out to the shop for the Sunday papers, or carrying a mug of coffee from kitchen to sitting room, he found his eyes straying up towards it. It made him uncomfortable.

At last, he went out into the garden on the pretext of making some plans for new borders and his vegetable patch. To his right, the old hedge between his own land and his neighbour's garden was high and thick, a tangle of *rosa rugosa* and privet and juniper. Much further down the garden, it thinned out a bit and it was there that he usually looked over and held friendly conversations with the elderly lady as she pottered about among her roses. He had given her his phone number.

'If you need anything, just give me a call,' he had told her, promising to come through and do some weeding for her, later in the spring.

But he could see nothing from this end, so close to the house. He stood outside his back door for a long time, listening, but he could hear only birdsong and the usual Sunday village sounds: a distant lawnmower, an occasional car, the excited mooing of cows let out to grass at last, the lazy drone of a small plane, practising aerobatics, high above the village. Nothing else. No voices at all.

Were they still kissing?

Unable to withstand his own gnawing curiosity he went back upstairs to the window, stood on the ladder and peered out again. He felt extraordinarily furtive, seeing without being seen. The couple were still together. There was a desperation about their caresses that he found both moving and distressing. Thoroughly ashamed of himself, he was about to descend and leave them to it, when he noticed a sudden, quick movement, just at the edge of the glass.

A third figure had come within the compass of his vision, another man he thought, from the general size and bearing. The newcomer was standing just behind the tree trunk, in an attitude uncomfortably suggestive of extreme tension. Indeed, the figure seemed at once furtive and yet poised as if ready to spring. As Jack watched, he saw the man raise a hand, a whole arm. But it was too long, too strong. He was holding something. What was it? A stick? Worse, an axe? He was stretching it up and out with a terrible tension about all his movements, a prelude to violence. It was the only interpretation Jack could place upon the gesture.

In an instant he had jumped from the ladder and was running down the stairs, out of the back door and into his own garden, shouting, 'Hey! Hey! Stop that!' But even before he reached the part of his garden where the hedge ran low enough to see over, he felt that something was wrong. Feeling foolish, he parted the leaves and peered back along the length of his neighbour's garden. It was quite empty. A well tended lawn gave way to a newly dug vegetable patch. Jack remembered that she had told him her grandson was coming round to do it for her. There was a little group of apple trees bunched up at the far end. It was as he had remembered. She had no cherry tree. No other trees at all.

He turned slowly back to his own garden, looking towards his cottage, seeking some explanation, but it too was basking innocently in the spring sunshine.

'How stupid to live in a place for six months and not to remember,' he thought, confused. His gaze slid across neglected flowerbeds to the rotting stumps of the old fence posts that had once marked the border between the two gardens, his own and the demolished cottage on the other side. There was no cherry tree in the garden of his own cottage. The gnarled old cherry stood in the middle of what had once been the lawn of the demolished house next door. He could see it now, with a pool of pink petals shed on the lengthening grass beneath.

He glanced up to his little round window. Not easy to see that garden from up there. Especially not when you were looking to the right. Impossible to see the cherry tree. Completely impossible.

The words dinned into his mind. His legs moved reluctantly as he retraced his steps back up to the window and peered out. The patch of grass beneath the cherry tree was quite empty now, the red glass turning the shed petals a vivid shade of crimson.

He had the window removed the very next day. He gave it back to Billy with his thanks, explaining that it made his hallway too dark.

'I think I'll just get some plain glass,' he said. 'Let a bit more light in.'

With what may be considered a remarkable lack of curiosity, Jack made no enquiries at all in the village as to the history of the demolished house next door to his own. He liked his cottage far too much for that. Better not to know what had happened. But when that year's flowering was over, he had the cherry tree chopped down and put up a bird feeder in its place.

'It only covers the lawn with dead petals,' he said, by way of explanation.

Some of the villagers thought it was a shame.

Others, older people for the most part, did not.

The Penny Execution

The saleroom was a last resort. Men are so difficult to buy Christmas presents for. It was well-nigh impossible to find anything original and entertaining for my husband but anyway, I walked up and down between the rows of furniture, the glass cases full of Doulton figures, Japanese vases and Staffordshire flatbacks, none of which Bobby finds particularly riveting.

Actually, I almost walked right past it. Perhaps I should have walked past it. Perhaps, on that bleak December day, I should never have gone to the saleroom at all, but I did, and I saw it and when I saw it, I had to have it. For Bobby, I told myself.

To tell the truth, I wanted it for myself as much as anyone else. That was why I was prepared to squander so much money on such a totally useless article. In retrospect, I find myself trying to read some sinister significance into that day, and the day after too, when I turned up at the saleroom, determined to outbid everybody. But in fact, there was nothing extraordinary at all, just the usual measure of acquisitiveness and passion and sometimes downright madness that salerooms can breed in bidders. Around me, I saw my own expression reflected in the shuttered, desiring faces of the dealers and maybe there *was* something a little sinister about that.

I had to have it.

And perhaps because the weather was very bad and no city

dealers had ventured out to our small town saleroom, and perhaps because it was too close to Christmas by now for the few local dealers to be sure of reselling, I managed to buy it. It was really much too expensive for me but not, I have since been told, too expensive for what it is. We have a collector from London coming to look at it today. With a bit of luck, he may buy it from us. We may even make a profit. We consider, Bobby and I, that we deserve a little compensation for wear and tear on our nerves.

So what was it, this object that I found so desirable at the time? It depends on how old you are, whether you will remember them or not. But back in the fifties and early sixties, there were still a number of them around. Oh they were old even then, of course. This was long before the advent of video games. In the amusement arcades back then, there would be a whole row of little glass and wood cases, inside each of which a three dimensional scene was depicted. It was usually a scene of horror. Sometimes it would be a haunted house, sometimes it would be a murder and sometimes an execution. You would put a penny in the slot in the machine – an old penny, that is – and suddenly the model would come to life, with a whirr and a click. In the haunted house, doors would spring open to reveal comical skeletons dangling jerkily behind them. The bed, complete with doomed occupant, would disappear. The murder was usually a gory one. The execution was sometimes a hanging, but often it was a beheading. And that was what I saw here in this small town saleroom, 'The Execution' painted flamboyantly across it, a detailed – albeit a little dusty – scene of a guillotine with a surrounding crowd.

I stared at it, fascinated, for a long time. I think it brought something of my childhood back to me. All at once, I remembered those trips to the seaside when I was so small that the sea looked massive and awe-inspiring. I remembered the amusement arcades with the grotesque Laughing Policeman and the little metal cranes that moved and caught precious prizes: whole fleets of plastic ducks, little baby dolls with painted hair, miniature packs of cards. Just for a moment, standing there in the saleroom, looking at the Execution, I was five years old again, smelling candy floss and shrimps and thermos flask tea.

So perhaps it wasn't all greed. Perhaps it was nostalgia as much as anything else. And knowing that Bobby would feel it too. I would like to think so. It would make me feel less responsible. But then it might also make me feel worse. You see, this collector is coming today all the way from London and I know he'll want to buy it and if I thought that my attitude in buying the thing had contributed in some way to what followed, I might feel safer about letting him go off with it. I have this idea that if he buys it out of love, everything might be alright.

Who am I fooling?

Certainly not myself.

'Does it work?' I asked the auctioneer.

'Yes. It's been rewired. I'll plug it in. There's a box of old pennies with it. You can keep using them. It's in good working order.'

He plugged the machine in, put a penny in the metal tray and pushed it in. We both stood back, the auctioneer and I, in the dark, cool, quiet saleroom, watching the glass box light up, watching the execution take place. It was rather horribly lifelike. There was an executioner, dressed all in black, standing by the guillotine and there was a tumbril – that's what they were called, isn't it? It was a sort of wooden wagon which came swaying out from behind a building. You couldn't tell where it had been hidden. A blindfolded prisoner stepped from it in a single fluid movement, knelt down and put his head on the block. Then the executioner raised his hand, a blade came flashing down, and the head fell off neatly into the basket provided for it. The headless body toppled over as well, and that was it. There was another whirr and a click and the light went out.

I shivered and the auctioneer looked at me and laughed. 'Good, isn't it?' he said. 'If a little macabre!'

'Pretty good,' I agreed. 'My husband would love it. Where did it come from?'

'Oh, lurking in somebody's attic. Long forgotten. We were doing a house clearance. Maybe some family member had an amusement arcade.'

'I wonder who made it?'

He shrugged. 'I don't know. But they must have made quite a lot of them at one time. It's Edwardian, I think. Possibly even older. I doubt if he ever saw a real execution in his life, though!'

I remember him saying that, because now I find myself wondering about it. Well, whoever made it, if he never saw an execution in his life, he must have had a pretty good imagination. It's funny how we use that word so dismissively. 'Imagination,' we say. 'Just your imagination,' whenever we see or hear something out of the ordinary. Something inexplicable that disturbs or distresses us.

This collector, I wonder why he collects these things? These nasty little scenes. Do they feed his imagination, I wonder?

When I had bought it the next day, there was all the excitement of going to pick it up without Bobby knowing about it. We borrowed a friend's van and left the thing at my daughter's house. It went in their spare room and the box of pennies with it. I made it work for her, and she put a few pennies in it herself. We giggled about it, and I told her about those old fashioned seaside holidays I had enjoyed so much.

A few days before Christmas, when I had prepared a good hiding place for the peep-show at home, I went round to Sally's house to fetch it.

'I can't say I'll be sorry to see the back of it,' she said, casually and I thought at the time it was a strange thing to say. But when I asked why, she frowned and said, 'It's just David.'

David is her youngest, my grandson, ten years old and cheeky but cute.

I laughed. 'Has it been difficult to keep him away from it?'

'Quite the opposite,' said Sally. 'It scares the living daylights out of him. Video games and Doctor Who he can cope with but not your Execution. He looked at it once or twice, but after the last time, he wouldn't go near it again.'

'Why on earth not?' I asked, surprised.

'He said it was too real. It gave him nightmares. I've had to put a sheet over it. He said he kept thinking about it. I told him his imagination must be working overtime.'

I wonder how many children he has, this man who collects penny peep-shows. None, I hope.

Well, Bobby was delighted with his present, as I had known he would be. We spent most of Christmas morning shoving pennies into it and trying to see how the head got reunited with the body. We decided that it must be on a fine wire, must all spring back together again when the light went out. Bobby said he half wanted to take it to pieces and see how it worked, but I managed to restrain him, thinking about how much it had cost. Then we watched it all over again and gave it pride of place in the sitting room, right next to the Christmas tree. The more champagne we drank, the more we laughed at it. When the family, our grown up kids with their partners and children, descended on us in the afternoon, we watched it and laughed at it some more, all except young David, who wouldn't come in and look at it, but took his new bicycle out round the village until we had given up playing with it.

We actually thought it was the alcohol, you know. Sometimes, when you've had a bit too much to drink you begin to see things with a certain vividness, as if the colours have become brighter. Well, we began to look at the Penny Execution like that. In the evening, when our visitors had gone, Bobby said to me, 'You know when the blade comes down on the neck?' and I said, 'Well, what about it?' and he said, 'It looks as if there's blood on it.'

'No!' I said. 'You're imagining things.'

So we watched it again and sure enough, there was blood on the blade. It gleamed stickily in the illumination inside the box. But we could have sworn that it hadn't been there at the beginning of the scene, not when the prisoner came rolling up in the tumbril, so we had to watch it again and sure enough, the blade was clean and gleaming at first, with no blood on it at all. The blood came afterwards. After the execution.

'I wonder how it's done?' mused Bobby.

And I couldn't imagine. I just couldn't begin to imagine.

During Christmas week, we had plenty of visitors. We played the Penny Execution several times for all of them and we began to wonder if playing it over and over like that had got it working more smoothly. That seemed to be the only explanation for the small changes that began to come over it.

About the middle of the week, Bobby said, 'Is it my imagination, or is there a new figure in that scene, somewhere?'

I could hardly believe it, but sure enough, when I looked at it again, I saw somebody I hadn't noticed before. In the shadow of the guillotine and just behind the executioner, there was an old woman and she was knitting something black. Her hands moved, jerkily. I could have sworn she had just appeared. Bobby too. So the way we rationalised it to ourselves was this: through so many years of not being used, the works must have rusted up a bit, but now that we were using it so often, it was beginning to work better. We were seeing more of it. I could tell Bobby thought there was something not quite right about this theory, but he couldn't think of any better explanation and since he isn't a great believer in the power of the imagination, he had to make do with it.

The only way of knowing what was really going on in there would have been to take the thing apart and see exactly how it worked. And I wouldn't let him do that just yet. Not after what I had paid for it. 'Time enough for that,' I said, 'when it breaks down.' And if I'm honest with myself now, there was a little bit of me that hoped that it *would* break down. But the machine showed no signs of breaking down. In fact it went from strength to strength.

New Year's Eve was on a Saturday, that year. On Friday night, we noticed that some of the members of the crowd watching the execution had begun to move too, jerkily at first and then with astonishing fluidity. They shook their fists. They swayed from side to side. You could have sworn the expressions on the small faces had changed, had become livid with malice. You felt that – if it hadn't been for the glass case – you might even have heard their jeers.

But it was at New Year, just after midnight, that the Penny Execution gave its best – or worst – performance. There were plenty of people in the house. Word of the peep-show had got around and there were quite a few neighbours who had been away for Christmas. They had heard about it and come round to see what all the fuss was about.

'Go on then,' they said to Bobby. 'Let's see!'

And Bobby, hard headed, down-to-earth Bobby, said 'Do you really want to? Are you sure?'

He looked like David. I'll swear that if it had been possible, he'd have gone and ridden a bike around the village until it was all over.

But everyone said, 'Yes. Of course. Let's see the execution!'

The cry was taken up and chanted around the room. 'We want the execution! We want the execution!'

Bobby looked at them and shook his head, slowly. Then he shrugged, as if disclaiming all responsibility. I think I had begun to be afraid, even then.

Bobby slotted the penny into the machine. There were the familiar sounds and the bright, white light came on in the glass case. Then we saw the execution.

Only this time, there were three figures in the tumbril and one of them was a woman, her face bruised, her dress torn and her hair wild. The executioner dragged her out first and pushed her head down and the old woman carried on knitting the shapeless black woollen garment. I'd swear it had grown longer. The crowd moved restlessly. They waved their arms and mouthed insults and then the knife came swishing down. The body, the headless body, lay there, twitching in a pool of its own blood. There was blood on the axe and blood seeping out of the basket and – oh – perhaps I had been drinking too much. It was New Year after all. Except that Bobby saw it too. Everyone saw it. We talked about it a bit, much later on, too puzzled and scared to discuss it that night, all wanting desperately to deny the evidence of our own eyes. You see there were tiny drops of blood, splattered on the glass of the peep-show itself.

Our visitors went home soon after that and left us alone with our Penny Execution. We hardly talked about it. We covered it with a sheet and put it out in the garage and that's where it is now.

Today, there are snowdrops in the garden and a collector from London is coming to look at it. I'm almost sure he'll buy it. It's a highly desirable item. I know what I ought to do, of course. I ought to take the big axe that's kept out in the woodshed and chop the thing into little pieces and feed them into the Rayburn.

But I won't. And it isn't simply from any motive of greed. I am quite simply too scared to do it. Last night, Bobby said to me, 'I could always take it apart and see how it's made.'

I said, 'Do you want to?'

'Not for all the tea in China,' he said, with a shudder.

We can't keep it, of course. But we can't destroy it either. To give it away would rouse too many suspicions. I suppose I could have taken it back to the saleroom, but the auctioneer would be bound to ask questions. And I suspect he wouldn't want it either.

The last time I was in there, he said 'How are you getting on with your Penny Execution then?' And he winked at me.

I hear a car drawing up outside now. If the collector wants to see it working, I'll just have to go out and put the kettle on for coffee. Oh, it won't give him a complete performance. Not just yet. That isn't how it works.

But I hope and trust that he is a man of very little imagination.

Your Own Skipper

She sat on the beach, scuffing at the sand, her freckled face crimson with the heat. Her hair fell around her cheeks in fat red wedges. Her name was Margaret but everyone called her Mags. She and the boy, Jamie, had come from the city, first by train, then by bus and then on foot, out of the village and along the shore. She was already worn out by the journey although it was supposed to be an adventure, a holiday. She slipped off her sandy shoes and rubbed at her feet. She had left a suitcase in the bus station, bringing a straw bag packed with tissues, a bottle of Irn Bru for the boy, some crisps, a couple of oranges and a few other odds and ends. She had forgotten the sun cream but then she hadn't expected sunshine. Jamie was running in circles down by the sea, being something or other. Something on a horse. Suddenly he rolled over and over and stretched out. They'd got him. He got up slowly and came over to his mother, squatting down and resting both hands on her knees. His cheeks and hands were still a bit podgy but the rest of him was getting wiry. He was fining down. His knees were very bony and scarred below his shorts. He looked just like a small replica of his father, which worried her.

'I'm hungry, mum,' he said. 'I thought we were going to have something to eat in the village.' He gazed at her accusingly.

'There wasn't anywhere open.' She forced a smile. 'I've got crisps. And oranges.'

He held out his hand for a packet of crisps. She opened it for him.

'Don't gobble.'

It was what she always said.

He had been very quiet going through the village. Remembering that they had a few letting bedrooms, she had meant to get a room for them in the pub and then go back for their bags, but her courage had deserted her. She thought they might recognise her and she didn't want to engage in conversation. Not right at this moment. She had taken Jamie's unwilling hand and walked past the harbour, past the shop which had a closed sign on the door, through the rough grass and dunes to the sand.

'Well, what are we going to do then?' he persisted, squeezing her knees.

He was worried. His mum cried a lot. He was used to his dad not being there, hardly missed him at all now, but his mum worried him. He tried to tell her that he didn't mind about his dad, but she didn't understand him. Sometimes he wondered if it was something he had done, something bad that had driven his dad away. He would catalogue his small crimes, being cheeky, telling fibs, but it was like some huge question to which he could find no answer. Now, they had come to this strange place with its long, low houses, the sand, the sea that seemed scarily big. It made him dizzy just to look at it. She had told him that her grandparents, his great grandparents, had lived here, but they were dead now.

'Gone to heaven,' she said.

He wanted to say 'Well, why have we come here then?' but instead he asked again, 'What are we going to do?' He had eaten the crisps but he was still hungry and his legs were aching.

'Will we go back?' he asked fiercely.

'We'll go back to the village soon,' said Mags. 'We'll get somewhere to stay and something to eat. It'll be alright.'

Her eyes shifted from the sea with an effort. She found it difficult to want to move at all or even to focus on her son, but his discomfort was an imperative she couldn't ignore. She looked in the bag and found her purse, checking that her money and her bank card were there. She found half a Mars Bar, shapeless with the heat, and gave it to Jamie.

'But it'll make you thirsty.'

'We've got Irn Bru, haven't we?'

'I suppose so.' She looked around, squinting into the sunshine. 'It was always a nice place. My gran and grandad lived here. In that white cottage we passed, going over the bridge. They had the shop. Only it was all fisherfolk in the village back then.'

Jamie ate his chocolate with relish. 'Can I have an orange?'

'Can I have an orange what?' she asked mechanically.

'Can I have an orange please.'

Once, when his dad had asked him that, he had said 'Can I have an orange *now*?' and she had had to turn away to hide the smile. But his dad had not seen the funny side. 'Don't be cheeky. Or you'll feel my hand on your backside!'

Small transgressions. That's what she had wanted to say to him. Why do you take such small transgressions so seriously? But she didn't have the courage. Not then.

'Actually, you can't have an orange. You'll be sick. Wait a bit.'

He pulled a face, but didn't argue. He was, on the whole, an amenable little boy, doing as he was told.

'When I was young,' she said, 'When I was like you are now, I used to come here on holiday.'

'I liked the harbour. We could go back there. Soon. Look at the boats.'

There were only a few boats now, mostly small yachts, arranged like an illustration for a calendar. Picturesque Scotland. A single wooden boat with an outboard motor. Seafoam painted on the bow. Twenty years ago, the last time she had seen the village, there had still been a few fishing boats. It was a curious feeling, this going back to the time before she met her husband. Before Jamie. She could hardly remember life before Jamie. It was like trying to imagine life before you had arms or legs or a heart. Back then, there had been poles with nets hung on them. The fishermen still brought them back here from the town where most of their boats were berthed. But now they were gone. This part of the place had been gentrified. You weren't allowed to walk all the way around the harbour. Security for the yachts she supposed. There were large admonitory notices. Otherwise, the village hadn't changed much. It had spread out a bit, that was all. Like me, she thought.

'I'm really thirsty, mum.'

She got out the bottle of Irn Bru and they had a little drink each. 'Not too much,' she said. 'We'll get thirsty on the way back. It's quite a long walk.' She pushed her hair back from her face. She was wet under her arms. She sniffed at herself surreptitiously.

Jamie got up and wandered along the beach. Behind them was stunted woodland, the branches twisted by the prevailing wind. At the high water mark were shells, rotting turnips, empty plastic bottles, the spread-eagled feathers of a dead seagull. Flies hung over it in clouds. Mags turned her back on the dead bird and sat on a stretch of flat sand, dotted with smooth stones, close to the sea. To the north, the village lay out of sight behind cliffs and fields. South, the sand was shot with winkle pools, ragged with seaweed and wrecked wood. Further along the beach, steps were cut into the rock and a house sat high up, squat and square. Jamie had moved to the south end of the bay, looking for crabs. She got up and followed him. He disappeared behind an outcrop of rock just as she caught up with him, and she had to peer over it to see him. Her constant low-key worry about him, occasionally elevated to an intense terror if he fell or was ill or even out of sight for too long, exhausted her. Nobody had told her it would be like this. She was sure it couldn't be normal. She couldn't let him see it, so she had to deal with it all the time. But controlling it took so much energy. So much effort.

The tide was still going out. He was standing with his hands behind his back, watching a man who was bent almost double, gathering winkles into a black plastic bucket.

'What are they?' he asked. 'Can you eat them?'

The man looked up. He wore a navy blue jersey, faded jeans and big boots. 'I hope so,' he said. The corners of his eyes crinkled. Mags saw that he was shy rather than dangerous.

'Come away and don't bother the gentleman,' she said.

The man looked up at her and his face lit up with recognition. The words just came into her head because it was like a sudden illumination, his eyes wide, his mouth opening in a big grin.

'Mags!' he said.

'Ally.'

She knew him but he looked so much older than she remembered him that she was disconcerted. He seemed glad to see her.

'It's been a long time!' he said.

'I'm surprised you recognised me.'

'Is this your – ?'

'My son. Yes. Jamie.'

'You must come to the house. Come up with me to the house,' he said.

Twenty years ago, she had been fifteen, staying in the white house over the bridge. Her grandparents had taken her along to a ceilidh in the village hall. Fundraising for some local good cause. There had been a gap between visits because they had been living in the south. But her father's work had brought him back to Scotland. Ally was there, leaning uneasily against the wall, smiling. Smoking. You could still smoke in public places back then. He couldn't have been more than twenty five but he seemed old to her, the way adults seem old when you're fifteen.

'Ill luckit Ally,' said her grandad, and her grandma whispered fiercely, 'Hush now. The old man's over there.'

'What's that?' Mags asked, interested.

'Ally's father, Jimmy,' said her grandma. 'Best fisherman of his day. And those *were* the days. He's a friend of your grandad.'

Mags remembered Jimmy, very broad about the middle, his hair already a white halo. Later, in the lavatory, her grandma said, 'They say Ally's unlucky. Won't have him stepping over the nets and that. Some of them's that superstitious they'd be feart to meet their own mother coming down to the harbour. But Jimmy lost a man overboard. Tommy Scobie. Just a young lad. Well, that finished it. Jimmy never went back to the fishing. And they say he spoiled Ally for it. But I'll not believe that. He was aye feckless as a lad was Ally.'

Grandma hurried back to the dance. Mags didn't believe in superstition but she looked curiously at Ally. Later, her grandma had introduced her to Ally and his father. 'This is my grand-daughter, Margaret.'

'Mags. Everyone calls me Mags.'

'Peggy's girl?' asked Jimmy, stretching out his hand. 'I mind your mother when she was wee. You're very like her.'

Her grandma moved away to speak to Jimmy. The air was smoky, the music loud and slow. Ally said awkwardly, 'Will you dance?' He put out his cigarette and lead her onto the dance floor.

'I should give up the smoking,' he said.

'I can't dance at all. Not this kind of dancing, anyway.'

'Neither can I,' he said. 'Feet too big.'

They shuffled around the floor but presently, when they began to talk to each other, their movements became less self-conscious. He was undemanding and kind.

'Where do you live?' she asked.

'Just south of here. In the house along the beach. With my father.'

He told her she must come and visit them some time. When the music stopped, he lead her to her seat and thanked her courteously. It made her feel very grown up. She wished he would dance with her again, pretending to herself that she liked him more than she did, but that was the last she saw of him for twenty years. She remembered how in the village they had always called the cottage the 'winkle picker's house' and that was Ally. It was what he did most of the time. He gathered shellfish from the shore and sold them to local restaurants. Sometimes he put out a few creels for crabs and lobsters. It was a living of a sort.

Now, she walked up to the house with him with Jamie running and jumping around them, excited to be going somewhere, anywhere. Inside, she hardly recognised the old man hunched morosely beside an empty hearth. The years had not been kind to him. He looked thin and ill, but he managed a smile for Jamie. 'You've got the same name as me,' he said.

'Have I?'

'Only everyone calls me Jimmy.' He stretched out a hand and Jamie shook it gravely.

Jimmy looked with concern at Mags who was feeling very dizzy, what with the sunshine and the hunger.

'You don't look well, lass. Sit down now. Sit yourself down.'

'Don't let us bother you, please.'

She was agitated, as much by his appearance as anything else. She had remembered him as sturdy, good humoured. Now he had shrunk. He saw her gazing at him and, sitting up very straight, he took his pipe out of his pocket and began to fill it.

'Where will you be staying then?'

'I thought I'd take a room over the pub for a few days.'

'Oh it's not what it was, that place. It's a rough place these days, hen. No place for a wee lad.'

Ally made tea and poured it out. He had cut thick slices of

white bread, butter and jam, and put them on a plate. He gave Jamie the first cup, baby tea with plenty of milk and sugar. Then he winked at Mags over the teapot. She ate greedily and felt better. Jimmy cleared his throat and drank a mouthful of tea. He looked at a point somewhere over Mags's left shoulder and said, 'Why don't you both stay here for a while?'

'Well it's very kind of you to offer, but we couldn't.'

'Why not? There's plenty of room. And the pub isn't a good place. Well, not to stay. There are a couple of farm guest houses but you'd need a car. You should stay here.'

It was tempting, mainly because she didn't want to have to go anywhere else. Not today, not now.

'Are you sure?'

'Your grandparents would never forgive us if we let you stay in the pub. Old friends that we are. It's not very comfortable there either. None too clean these days.'

While Ally fetched their luggage from the bus station, Jimmy insisted on helping her to make up the bed. He looked too frail to be doing it but it was clear that the men were pleased to be looking after her. The old man always slept downstairs in a back bedroom. The lavatory was downstairs and if he had to get up in the night Ally didn't want him falling, so he told her.

Upstairs there were two big bedrooms. Mags and Jamie could share a double bed. She didn't mind. She liked to sleep with her son, loved to feel the curve of his little body inside the protection of her arms, liked to hear his quiet breathing in the night. Jimmy had been one of a large family and after a particularly good period of fishing they had moved to the house from one of the village cottages. Outside, there was a hut for storing nets, now full of ancient, rotting gear: lines and seines and old lobster creels all jumbled together. Ally's mother was dead. His elder sister and younger brother had long ago left the village: one to marriage and a settled city life, the other to a lucrative job on the rigs. Jimmy was disappointed. He had wanted one fisherman son at least. A son-in-law would have done. He had never meant to finish with the sea altogether but he never had considered Ally to be a fisherman either. He had always thought his middle son peculiarly impractical. Too slow, too shy. There had always been some sickness of defeat in Ally's manner. He never fought back. Besides, the fishing was all but finished now. Destroyed by a string of false promises. So perhaps Ally was right. Perhaps it was drawing to a close.

Young Jamie was bewildered by it all at first, then suddenly happy.

'Just a wee holiday,' his mother told him. But days soon became weeks. It was July and Mags didn't have to think about school for him. He would spend hours with Jimmy, walking along the shore, examining rock pools, scrambling away from the old man and returning sooner or later to show his treasures: stones, shells, feathers. But he gravely declined all Ally's offers of a trip aboard the Seafoam. When Mags questioned him about it, wondering why he wouldn't want to help Ally with his creels, he said, 'He's not safe, you know. He's ill luckit.'

She laughed in spite of herself. 'Says who?'

'His dad told me. Jimmy. He said Ally's no fisherman.'

'That's not very kind, is it?' she said.

She remembered Jamie coming in from school with a drawing, proud of himself. 'What's that supposed to be,' her husband had said. 'Is that supposed to be a person? Think you need a few more lessons, son.'

Thoughtlessly cruel.

Ally was still pathologically shy. It was useless to try to draw him out. He was most inclined to speak when they were sitting quietly in the evening, when his father and her son had gone to bed. Sometimes he listened while she talked. He was a good listener.

Ally made his own creels, cleverly, in the old fashioned way, netting the covers himself and fixing them over bent hazel rods. He was very adroit, for somebody who was meant to be impractical. She liked to watch him working away in the quiet shed with the sun filtering in the dusty windows.

'I wish Jamie would come and watch you,' she said. 'He might learn something.'

'Ach – ' He pulled at the netting needle. 'Who would want to learn this? What good would it be? Leave the wee lad alone. He tells me this isn't real fishing at all.'

'Oh?'

'Aye.' He smiled good naturedly. 'I should have lived a hundred years ago. You'll have to watch Jamie though. He'll be away on the trawlers before you know what he's about. Or what's left of them these days. Maybe the rigs instead. What's left of *them*.'

'Not Jamie. That's not what I want for him at all.'

'He's been listening to my dad. But he's right. It's not the industry it was. Maybe he could join the navy.'

The idea of her son on a trawler or even at sea disturbed her. She watched him later as he fixed glowing, delighted eyes on Uncle Jimmy.

The days grew more sultry. It was the best summer for years on this coast. Still she did nothing but read, cook and wash out clothes for herself and Jamie. The men had their own routine and she didn't disturb it.

'We like having you here, so we do!' said Jimmy.

The squall which marked the end of the hot spell came on the same evening that the Seafoam's engine stopped dead, just off the bay, with its jagged arms of rock: thunder, lightning, a sudden wind and a sheet of rain.

'It's not a coast,' Jimmy had told Mags, 'To be running in on with your engine broken down.'

Clouds tumbled across the skies like a flock of crazed sheep. The wind howled madly and unseasonably, tearing leaves, rattling rain down the chimney. Jamie ran in, crying out for her. She took him in her arms but he shouted at her, 'He's going to wreck the Seafoam. He's going to wreck her!'

Jimmy struggled into his coat and walked up the hill behind the beach with Jamie trailing after him. They went to watch Ally fighting with the silent engine and the wild sea, riven by the occasional lightning strike. Jamie clutched at the old man's hand, too scared to cry. Mags stayed in the house, walking around, touching things, lifting them up and putting them down again, the clock, the kettle, the china dogs beside the fireplace. She went out to the shed and sat on Ally's bench breathing in tar and fish smells.

Then, quite suddenly, the squall began to abate and the sun came out, low on the horizon, turning the clouds pink and gold. Some metres away from disaster, as if in acknowledgement of the anti-climax, Ally kicked the engine into life and brought the boat safely into the bay. They all helped him to haul it onto the sand. The old man kept his hand on Ally's shoulder for a long time.

'Don't you ever do that to me again, son!' he said. 'Don't ever do it again.'

Later, Mags heard the scrape of spade on sodden, stony soil. She went out into the garden and saw that Ally was digging there.

'Why on earth are you digging in the dark?' she asked. 'You can't dig wet earth like that. Haven't you done enough for one day, nearly getting yourself killed?'

He stopped, stuck the spade in the earth. 'I was only going after lobsters,' he said, mildly. 'Lifting my creels. It's what I do. I can't settle though. Not tonight. I thought I might get some worms.'

'You ought to stick to winkles.'

That was cruel. Everything in him shrank from the discipline of a bigger boat and from the constant exposure to others and their sharp words.

'I pushed her too hard. The bloody old boat. I pushed her too hard.'

Mags wanted to tell him how glad she was that he wasn't drowned or even injured. Instead she said briskly 'Well, come in and have a cup of tea.'

On the way in, her hand brushed his arm.

'Sorry,' he said, as if it were his fault.

He was very big and cool in spite of his exertions. His trousers bagged slightly at the back. She wanted him to touch her. They sat in the kitchen, drinking strong tea. Mags found that her hands were shaking. Ally was smoking and staring at the cupboards over the sink. His eyelids began to droop with fatigue. He took off his jersey and his hair stood on end like his father's. She watched his crooked face until his eyes flickered open. He smiled uncertainly.

'You should be in bed,' she said.

'I should.' He stubbed out his cigarette. 'You sound like my mother.' He rubbed his fingers over the frayed cuff of his working shirt. They stood up. He locked the door and she switched off the light. They climbed the stairs. On the landing, she took his hand and touched it against her cheek.

'I'm so glad you're safe.'

They stumbled against each other clumsily. His feet were in the way of hers. She kissed his cheek and then his lips. He was trembling, his whole body shaking. He smelled of tobacco. His skin tasted of salt.

'Is that you, mum?' called Jamie. 'Can I have a drink of juice?'

They parted, Ally to his own room, Mags to soothe her son, fetch him a drink, creep in beside him.

Young Jamie and old Jimmy went walking along the seashore. Jamie was swaggering in new trainers, a gift from Ally.

'I don't want to be a winkle picker,' he said.

Jimmy looked down at him. 'You'll not. No. You'll never be that.'

'I want to be a real fisherman. A skipper on a big trawler. A big prawn boat maybe. And make a lot of money.'

'I don't know that anyone makes a lot of money at the fishing these days, son. Not unless they own the bloody boat. But I suppose you could work on a boat. Be a yacht skipper even. You'd have to work hard though. Learn all about the sea. It's a dangerous place. You can't afford to take any chances with the sea.'

'Then I'll buy mum a house and you can have a new car and oh, anything you want.' He paused. 'Uncle Jimmy? Why isn't Ally a proper fisherman?'

Jimmy knocked out his pipe on a rock. 'He made his own bed and now he lies on it. But maybe I'm just hard on him. I was afraid for him and that's the truth.'

Drowned Tom Scobie came into his mind, just a youngster, newly come on the boat. They hadn't found the body for months, long after the memorial service. He remembered Scobie's wife and how she had looked drowned and dead too. He had never set foot on a boat after. But he regretted it now. He should not have turned his back on the sea like that. It had been the wrong decision. But he couldn't say any of that to the wee lad, could he?

'You see, Ally never wanted more than just a small boat like the Seafoam and the occasional crab and lobster. He wasn't too bothered with anything else. I suppose I wanted more for the lads. Too much maybe. I wanted a skipper for a son. Other fellows, well, they go out on their son's and their grandson's boats when they're older.' His voice rose querulously and he was disgusted with himself. 'Don't mind me,' he said. 'I'm just a daft old man. Don't mind me.'

'You can go out on my boat when I get her, so you can,' said Jamie.

Ally sat beside the fire, a netting needle in his hand. He had had his hair cut and the nape of his neck looked naked and vulnerable. It reminded Mags of her son.

She said, 'Ally, I'm going to have to go away.'

'I thought you might say that sooner or later.'

She wanted to shake him. Why did you think that? Why can't you tell me how you feel?

She couldn't bring herself to say it. Instead she said, 'Do you want me to go?'

'You must do what you want.' His head drooped and his hands hung miserably between his knees.

'What about what *you* want? Do you want anything at all?' she asked.

He shook his head. 'Are you going back to him, then? Your husband?'

'No. He wouldn't want us. And I certainly don't want *him*. I'm just going to have to make my own way. Jamie deserves better than this.'

She didn't know what else to say. He bought gifts for Jamie but there was nothing for her. No words of affection or even encouragement. Nothing. She thought perhaps he was afraid. But what could she do about that?

'You'll take Jamie then?'

'What on earth do you mean?'

'I was thinking of the old man. They're friends.'

'I suppose they are. But I can't help that, can I?'

Mags got up, rocking the chair as she did so. She turned to the door and could hardly see it because of the tears in her eyes.

Jamie was running in circles down by the sea, hauling one of the bags after him. Mags struggled with the bigger case. Ally had gone out in the Seafoam very early and they thought the old man was still asleep. In fact he had lain in bed and heard them go, then got up and watched from an upstairs window. He went downstairs and made a cup of tea, strong and sweet. He didn't want Ally to come home. He couldn't cope with it.

On the beach, Jamie said to his mother, 'I'm going to be a fisherman you know.'

'We'll see.'

'I don't care what you say. I am.'

'Not like Ally. Not like him.'

'I didn't say that.'

Far away round the headland they could see the black speck that was the Seafoam. Jamie watched it with narrowed eyes. 'Not a wee boat like that. A big one. One that goes far out and makes a lot of money. What's the good of being your own skipper if you're the only one on the boat?'

He ran down to the sea and stuck his tongue out at the horizon. Mags was afraid for him. She felt the love and fear twisting inside her. Why had nobody told her it would be like this? Who could imagine this pain? She put down the bags to change hands. In her mind's eye she saw Ally's gentle, tired face, saw him pushing his hair back with one big hand. She dismissed the image. She put it all from her mind, took up the cases and walked on.

Lip Reading

This train is for Ayr. Mind the gap. The young man is wrestling a massive suitcase aboard. It is a cheap affair that looks as though it may spring open at any moment, depositing his belongings onto the platform. The anticipation of this makes other passengers uneasy. This is a busy train, the five past five out of Central. He has missed the faster train by five minutes. They have a habit of leaving the announcement to the very last moment. People can never quite fathom why they do it. The train is always there when commuters rush and stumble onto this remote platform with seconds to spare. It looks as if it has been there for at least ten minutes, sighing and clicking quietly to itself. Sometimes the doors are locked, and the passengers pile up, shivering on the chilly platform, with the seconds ticking down until the driver arrives, in no very obvious hurry, and climbs aboard.

Mind the gap.

There isn't much room for luggage on this train, which is frustrating, since it stops both at Paisley, where people alight for Glasgow Airport, and further down the line at Prestwick International Airport. There are times of day when the train is crammed with travellers, all struggling with luggage. It blocks the aisles and prevents new arrivals from sitting down.

The young man is Polish and his name is Anton. He is dressed in a navy blue sweater, pale and slightly grubby tracksuit bottoms, a hooded top. He sits, jiggling his knees and staring at his phone as though willing it to ring, but it stays silent. He has dark hair, cut close to his scalp, a thin face, button brown eyes like a teddy bear and an anxious expression. He seems to be trying hard to listen to the conversations going on around him, perhaps to understand them, but he doesn't realise that this makes him look intrusive, his eyes flickering from face to face. It makes him look as though he is lip-reading. People gaze back at him resentfully, and he subsides into his seat, staring out of the window, letting the foreign words wash over him.

He has been in Scotland for a few of years and in that time his English has improved a little, but not much. He has been working in Glasgow as a kitchen porter, sharing a flat in a tower block with a number of other young Poles. Sometimes, if they are working shifts, they sleep in shifts as well, two or three of them in the same bed, the sheets smelling of other people's sweat. The flat is mouldy. There are scuffs on the skirting boards, holes in the walls, cigarette burns on the vinyl, mice in the kitchen. The windows with their flimsy curtains drawn seem warmer and better insulated than the outside walls. The stairwells, full of graffiti and the smell of pee, are haunted by confrontational young Scots. Foreigners climb the stairs in threes because it seems safer. It is no colder than Poland, no colder than Krakow, but it is certainly more damp. He has been sad all the time but waking up in the mornings has been the worst. At night, after a beer or two, he can feel the weight of misery lifting from him. In the mornings, he has to force himself to get out of bed.

It occurs to him that he has been homesick. He didn't know just how homesick until this moment, when he senses a measure of blessed relief, a lifting of his spirits. And all because he is on the train, on his way to the airport, with his massive case resting against his knees. He relaxes, listening to the conversations around him, trying hard to understand.

They spoke Polish at work and Polish at the flat. They shopped in Aldi or Lidl or sometimes in Polish delis, coming home with familiar food: tins of bigos and sauerkraut, packets of kabanos sausage, rye bread with caraway seeds, foil wrapped Wawel chocolates from Krakow with names like *Kasztanki* and *Kokosowe*. Krakow is his home town. In Glasgow, he had signed on with a temporary employment agency, going wherever he was sent: sometimes to company canteens, occasionally to a private school. On one of their infrequent nights out, in a bar in Sauchiehall Street, he met a young teacher from the school. She spoke to him, flirted with him, but the next time he saw her in the school she ignored him as if he were a non-person.

Often, he worked in one of the city's big football stadiums, but he liked those jobs least of all. The kitchen porters were supposed to be invisible. The paying customers were not meant to be aware of their existence. This was what it must have been like to be a servant in a pre-war country house. The customers were a mixed bunch. Some of them looked as though they might once have been kitchen porters themselves, long ago in another life, although now they were heavily disguised in flashy suits and shiny shoes.

The work was hard, but he didn't mind. He could haul sacks of potatoes and crates of bottles about with ease. He could carry trays of dishes, thrusting them into and pulling them out of the industrial dishwasher, with the steam and the chemicals burning his nostrils while the chef roared at them, partly in frustration at not being able to make himself understood, but partly – Anton sometimes thought – because he too might be sick of his job. They were all afraid of him. '*Zwariowany!*' they would say. 'Crazy. Nutter.'

At first, he thought that he might be able to improve his English, sign up to evening classes, but when he enquired about them he found that they were far too expensive, once he had paid his tax and his council tax, his rent and his food, and sent a little money home to his mother and his grandmother. The words and phrases he learnt at work, get that effin tray over here ya wee bastard, clear that effin mess up, were not, he felt, words that would stand him in good stead in any but the most limited circumstances. Besides that, the work made him feel ill. He couldn't understand why, because he had been used to hard work in the past. He wasn't sure whether it was the chemicals or the heat, the lack of fresh air or his exposure to unfamiliar viruses, but he had contracted a string of colds and minor infections. Now, he has spots on his chin, eczema on his hands and in his ears. He has been sleeping badly and keeping himself awake half the night, coughing. He has tried not to tell his mother about all this, but she can always hear it in his voice on the phone, and he knows that she worries about him.

On the train, he gazes out of the window towards the hills which are dusted with snow. He would like to have travelled out of the city, to have been able to walk in the countryside, explore the hills, but there never seemed to be time, nor was there enough money, and everything was difficult. He feels disappointed in himself for his lack of enterprise, his lack of energy. It feels like a missed opportunity. He and his flatmates went to Edinburgh on the bus one day and walked up and down the Royal Mile but they couldn't even afford to go in the castle. In Glasgow, they visited the Kelvingrove Museum because it was free, but it was full of schoolchildren rushing from place to place, their cries bouncing off the high ceilings. The walls were covered, not just in paintings, but in words he couldn't understand. Words that he assumed would tell him what to think about the pictures. Why, he wondered? What was the point of pictures if somebody had to explain what they meant? In summer, he and a few friends would catch this same train to Ayr, finding their way down to the beach, where there was nothing to do but walk along the sand, eat ice cream or chips, and watch the girls watching them. Once, he went to the Botanical Gardens, by himself, walking along Great Western Road to get there, unsure of which bus to take. He wandered through the Victorian glass houses, enchanted by the colour and the scent of the flowers there. Then he sat outside for a long time in the sunshine, watching a crow as it rummaged for insects among heaps of cut grass. It was, perhaps, his happiest day in Scotland.

He has spent some time trying to reconcile this country and its people with the Scotland about which he had heard from his grandfather. Stefan had come here towards the end of the war. He had been lucky to survive. They all knew that. Stefan had been one of those who fell foul of Stalin and was imprisoned in Russia. To Anton, it seems faintly unreal, like a film, but back then it would have been fraught with terrible dangers. Stefan had risked cholera, typhus, dysentery and summary execution. When Stalin changed sides, Stefan had been released, joining the Polish Second Corps, and had come to Scotland by way of Italy. That too had been fraught with terrible dangers. 'Red are the poppies on Monte Cassino,' Stefan had sung when he had had a bit too much to drink and the tears had run down his cheeks, embarrassing his grandchildren. Stefan had been stationed in Fife until his unit was demobbed. He had loved the place. The people were friendly. They were kind to the Poles. Everyone, well almost everyone, knew that millions of Poles, soldiers and civilians, had died in the war, that the Poles were brave, that Polish pilots had fought and died in the Battle of Britain. The young Scotswomen were charmed by these ultra polite incomers who were as likely to kiss your hand as shake it and if the young Scotsmen were less than pleased about this, well, it was understandable.

Stefan could have stayed on in Scotland. He had been offered work in Fife near the camp where he had been stationed. There was a farmer called John McNair whose only son had died in the war. He had offered Stefan a job, growing vegetables at his farm near Kingskettle, on the flat lands of the Howe of Fife. Stefan had been tempted. It might have been possible, especially since he came from a farming background. He knew how to grow carrots, cabbages and potatoes. He might have done well. But he had a young wife in Poland, and they had lost touch during the upheavals of the war years. He didn't know whether she was dead or alive, but he couldn't rest until he found out. So he had gone home in search of her, although many of his countrymen had remained in Scotland. He had found her and couldn't help but be glad of it, although times had been very hard in Poland, especially while Stalin was still alive. Stefan had kept his head down, but had been lucky not to finish up in prison or in Siberian exile, branded a spy or a traitor because of his time abroad. Stefan had loved the Scots but he was not so complimentary about Churchill or Roosevelt who, he would say repeatedly, 'sold us down the river. They just sold us down the river!' Anton could remember his father standing behind Stefan, mouthing the words along with him, smiling ruefully. Sold us down the river.

Stefan was dead now, but when Anton was a little boy, he had listened, enthralled by stories of Scotland, the fertile fields of Fife, the castles, the music that was, in a way, like Polish music, the food which – also like Polish food – involved large helpings of bread, potatoes, cabbage and meat. But then there were the strange names, the smoky taste of whisky, the people who were not like Poles at all, who were much more reserved but friendly when you got to know them.

'The Scots understand the Poles. We understand each other. We have things in common. Difficult neighbours, for one.' That was what Stefan always said.

Anton doesn't think that is true these days. Anton thinks they have almost nothing in common, Poles and Scots.

It's true that the Scots are less than happy about their neighbours. Plenty of evidence of that. All around him he sees and hears people talking about a 'better Scotland'. He assumes they mean better without England in the way that Poland is better without Russia. And there are jokes, just as Poles tell jokes about the Russians. Who's to say they are wrong? He can understand why the crowds in the pub will cheer for Poland rather than England when they are watching a football match, even when it's clear that they don't like the Poles much either. Not in the flesh. Not when they are here, in Scotland. 'Taking our jobs,' they say. Friends tell him that it is much worse for Poles in England now. And not getting any better. They like the work the Poles do, just wish they could be invisible while doing it.

At first, he didn't understand what people were saying to him, but now he does. Once he was physically assaulted by an old woman when he was coming out of the Polish shop with his few groceries.

'Get back home!' she had said to him, belabouring him with her handbag, while he tried to fend her off. 'Get back to where you belong.'

It would have been comical if it wasn't so unexpected, so disturbing. Her face had been frightening, contorted with rage. There had been people standing nearby, waiting for a bus, studiously avoiding the confrontation. She moved away, leaving him trembling with a mixture of shock and suppressed rage. Only a middle aged woman stopped. 'Don't listen to her, son. Don't you pay any attention to her.' She patted his arm briefly, calming him down. It was the first time anyone from Scotland had made any kind of voluntary physical contact with him.

Brexit had only made things worse. He was supposed to apply to stay here, but it started him wondering if he wanted to stay here at all. The stories from his friends and colleagues, especially those living and working in England, grew more worrying. 'Speak English!' 'Go back where you belong!' 'Now we'll get rid of the lot of you.'

Sinister, hurtful things. Once, he heard about a young Polish man who had asked for directions in a London bus station and been beaten up for no reason at all.

'You're lucky you're in Scotland,' one of his friends told him on the phone. 'They don't want us here.'

'I don't think they want us here either,' he had said, aware as he said it that perhaps his friend was right. Perhaps things were better in Scotland after all.

On the train, Anton, silently forms the words 'mind the gap', moving his lips. For several months now, he has been thinking about going home. If he is honest, he has been thinking about going home for more than a year, but in the past few months, the desire has crystallised into an intention and then into a craving so acute that it is a physical pain, tightening his chest, shortening his breath. When he saw the exclamatory government adverts exhorting him to apply to stay, a kind of lethargy had set in for a while. Then he had asked himself if he actually wanted to stay where he was so clearly not wanted, and the answer had been of course not, who would?

He gazes at a middle aged man and woman sitting diagonally opposite. They stare back at him, impassively. They have been shopping and are surrounded by carrier bags. The last time his mother wrote to him, she wondered why he wouldn't come home. Things were pretty good now economically, if not politically. There was no need for him to be working as a kitchen porter in a hostile foreign country. Perhaps he would be able to study and hold down a job at the same time. And later, perhaps he could find a better job somewhere closer to home. Besides, his grandmother was missing him and she was a little frail. Reading between the lines, he realises that his grandmother is very frail and his mother is afraid that she will die before he can come home. The closer he has come to his departure date, the more he has worried about it, but now, he will be home before midnight and his grandmother is still alive. Quite well, all things considered. He feels as though he is willing the train on, the way he pedalled his bike when he was a little boy. Hurry up, hurry up, he thinks.

For some reason, he had expected more of this country and its people, after all his grandfather told him. He had not expected what he found here. How foolishly optimistic to expect people to be different. He is glad that his grandfather is no longer alive to ask him about it. What would he have said? Would he have smiled and lied? Or would he have said that the Scots were exactly like everyone else: some good, some bad, and most of them given to exaggerating their own virtues at the expense of everyone else. Stefan would have been disappointed.

The truth is that it might have been bearable. He might have applied for settled status, even though he didn't feel very settled, might have stayed a bit longer. But it was the conversation he had in one of the kitchens that finally made him borrow a laptop, go online, buy a ticket from Prestwick to Krakow, and call his mother.

It was seventy five years after the liberation of Auschwitz and the television had been full of commemorative programmes. He has an uncle who was born in Oswiecim, the town, not the camp. It was a pretty place, the old town, with a market square and handsome churches. But whenever anyone asked Uncle Tadek where he came from, he knew that they would flinch at his reply.

'Somebody has to come from there,' he would say, mildly.

They would ask him if the story about the birds not singing was true. He would say that he didn't know, but he could imagine that it might be true, although the birds sang in the town, right enough. Plenty of them. He knew because he fed them. Tadek's great aunt had been imprisoned in the camp, because she had been married to a Polish army officer. The Poles were not, as a rule, sent to the gas chambers. But they were non-people, all Slavs were. She had survived for a while, but then she had fallen very ill and been sent to Bergen Belsen and died there right at the end of the war, one of thousands shovelled into mass graves, a jumble of arms and legs, like so much detritus.

What troubled Anton then, what troubles him still, is the reaction of the young Scotsmen working in the kitchen alongside him. The way newspapers and television spoke about Polish death camps. The way his co-workers, taking their cue from such reports and, ignorant of history themselves, had asked him about his grandfather.

'So which side did Poland fight on in the war anyway?' one of them asked. 'You say your grandad was here. Was he wan o they Nazis then? A lot of those prisoners of war stayed on afterwards, didn't they?'

The rational, sensible part of his mind knew that such ignorance was a failure of education. But his own visceral rage took him by surprise. He did not have the words then. He does not have the words now. He stares at the people in the railway carriage, trying to understand their swift repartee. He kicks at the rigid blue case, willing the train on, needing to be home. He wonders what they are saying, following the movements of their mouths. Mind the gap.

Civil Rights

She liked everything about the city from the scent of fresh coffee and yeast buns that drifted out of Bewley's in the mornings, when she passed it on her way to work, to the sluggish Liffey reflecting the lights by night. She loved the quiet gallery where, on her days off, she could stand and stare at the jewelled panels of Harry Clarke's stained glass. She loved the smoky pubs and the voices of the people, those hard edged tones that were the same in all big cities where people had once had to make themselves heard above the din of machinery and traffic and politics.

But if she loved Dublin, she hated her work, a vacation job found for her by one of her father's colleagues. She worked in a gloomy office, its windows so high that you couldn't see out of them. The company dealt in animal feedstuffs and she sat at a desk in a room full of other girls. On each desk was a clumsy calculator that regurgitated a strip of flimsy paper. She would type tons, hundredweights, pounds and ounces into it. Then came prices in pounds, shillings and pence. And then she would do arithmetic and fill in complicated forms. It was 1969 and computerised calculators, if they existed at all, were so large that they filled rooms. Girls came cheaper.

Afterwards, it struck her that she must have got many of the calculations wrong. The job was so boring that getting the calculations wrong seemed like a necessity, staving off misery with small acts of revolution. She sat at the back and worked away with every appearance of diligence, and a man with a grim face sat in front, facing them, like a schoolmaster at his desk, watching them. If they talked he would shout at them, but she seldom talked to anybody and never got shouted at. She was an incomer and largely ignored. She didn't mind too much. She just got on with creating arithmetical mayhem, and left at the end of the day for the hostel up at St Stephen's Green, with its vapid statues in every alcove. It was part of a convent and it was run by the nuns. No men were allowed in the building, never mind in any of the rooms. Sometimes she would get dressed up and go out for the evening with the girls from her shared room and sometimes she would wander about the city all by herself.

Then, a few weeks into her summer, she saw a poster advertising a civil rights meeting in the centre of Dublin. The year before, her first year at university, she had started going to Irish civil rights meetings in Edinburgh. Everyone associated with the movement seemed to have a certain glamour about them, whether it was the handsome professor, who told them about Irish History or passionate Bernadette Devlin, or the friend of a friend who talked casually about the state of affairs at home and how something had to change sooner or later and it might as well be now. On her way to Dublin, she had travelled through Larne and Belfast. It seemed – as it undoubtedly was – another country with its big bright King Billy murals and its union flags everywhere. She had never seen so many flags in all her life.

That Saturday in Dublin, she went to the meeting and mingled with the crowd. She listened to speeches, and felt as if she was part of something meaningful and exciting. Somebody tapped her on the shoulder and when she turned round she saw that it was the friend of a friend from university. There were three of them, big, bold young men. They told her they had come down from the north and when they said that, they grinned at each other with a conspiratorial air. They said they couldn't go back over the border just yet, because things were very hot for them up there. Things would be a bit safer for them down here. They hoped. People noticed their accents, their northern voices and stared at them.

Later, the speeches grew more inflammatory, and the police who were lurking around the edges of the crowd became uneasy. Before the afternoon was over, the *gardai* had baton charged the crowd and people were running in all directions and screaming but she was safe enough because the boys from the north were much more watchful than the innocents from the south. They could see what was developing, could see what was about to happen and before the *gardai* made their move, one or them had seized her hand and said 'run!' They ran with her, pulling her down side streets, and they didn't seem to be afraid, in fact they were laughing as though it were a bit of a joke, not the real thing at all.

They went into a restaurant somewhere down by the river, a good restaurant, busy and full of tourists. They sat there, the three northerners and herself, and she saw that it wasn't the kind of restaurant she could ever afford to go to – her parents maybe, once in a while, but not herself on her student grant. She wondered who would pay, but she still belonged to an age when the man usually paid, especially if he was older, although not perhaps if he was a student. So she thought that they might pay for her, and if they didn't, then she had just enough money in her purse to pay for herself, if she was very careful what she ate, looking at the prices on the menu and choosing the cheapest things. One of the three was a big red headed, raw boned man, older than the others, and he wore dark glasses. Even in the restaurant, he didn't take them off and she noticed that he had bruises on his face. When he had tried to run, he had hobbled, and the others had been laughing at him, saying, 'Come on Liam, move your arse!' He sat opposite her and smiled at her, but he had a broken tooth and he looked as though he was in pain. She felt very sorry for him.

'What happened?' she asked and the others frowned, but he told her that he had been beaten up on his way home from a civil rights meeting, said that they must have been lying in wait for him, he hadn't stood a chance even though he was a big man and quite strong. But they had jumped him, three of them, and although he had managed to inflict a few bruises of his own, they had got him down in the end and kicked him where he lay. After that, they had decided to come over the border because things were looking a bit too hot to handle in the north. But Cork was where they ought to be, he said, not Dublin. Cork was the place to be, and she wondered why.

She knew Cork well, had worked in West Cork as an *au pair*, the summer when she was sixteen. 'Why Ireland?' somebody had asked and she had said it was because her grandmother was Irish which seemed reason enough. She thought of the place chiefly as a warren of fuchsia fringed lanes, mostly leading down to the sea. She had been looking after two year old triplets for an Irish family. They were holidaying in a flat in a run-down farmhouse. The rooms were dusty and her bed, in what had once been the maids' quarters, was lumpy and uncomfortable. Mice partied in the attics all night long. The little girls were funny and sweet but difficult. You could walk about with one under each arm, but then you would have to stagger after the third, who was always toddling off somewhere with great determination. Besides, there was a pig that would come crashing through the overgrown gardens, baring its yellow teeth, scaring the life out of you. The farmer's wife, Mary, took a liking to her and would invite her into the big kitchen for tea. She would cut thick slices of corny bread, made with flour and soda and dried fruit, buttering the cut end of the loaf first, holding it in close against her chest and sawing at it with the bread knife. Her nana had made the same thing and cut it in the same dangerous way but she had called it teacake.

When the girls were asleep, she would go out to the dancing

in the village. A long driveway threaded through the neglected gardens of the house, between a profusion of buddleia flowers that drooped in the soft rain. For ever afterwards, she could never smell the honey scent of buddleia without remembering a boy called Michael who had kissed her on the driveway in the dark. All these things came into her mind at once, the scents and sounds and the remembrance of physical pleasure, when the red headed man talked about Cork. But she couldn't see why Cork was the place to be.

'A good place,' repeated the red headed man. 'Plenty of the lads down there.'

Not long after this, they got up from the table. One of them told her to head for the door, so she did, expecting that he would pay, wondering if she should offer to give him the money for her meal. But when they got to the door, the red headed man took her hand and said 'now we run!' and yanked her almost off her feet. Then they were running down the stairs and out into the street, and the other two were running after. They didn't stop until they were many streets away, leaning on each other and laughing. She was genuinely shocked and afterwards, for the rest of her time in the city, worried about it, worried that somebody would recognise her, wondered if she should go in and offer to pay for her meal, but it seemed an impossibility. Not her fault. And so she just let it go.

After that, they got a taxi, all chipping in for the fare. It stopped outside an old stone building that seemed to be divided into flats. They went up a narrow stair and knocked on a door. After a muttered conversation between the friend of a friend and somebody inside they were admitted to a shabby room. There was an ordinary wooden table and the smell of petrol was in the air, sickly and strong. She saw that the table was stacked with ranks of glass lemonade and wine bottles and funnels, like when her dad made wine on the kitchen table, but the bottles were full of something else. There were pieces of paper stuffed into the necks of them and trailing down the sides. She should have been afraid but she wasn't. There was an odd sort of excitement about it. But they didn't stay there long.

'Not safe', the red headed man said. 'They don't know what they're doing. And besides I need a smoke.'

'Christ, not in here!' somebody said, and they all laughed.

So they went out of the flat and down the stone stairs that smelled of pee and potatoes, and all the time they took her with them, as though she were one of them, as though she were part of the group. But still none of it seemed in any way real. Afterwards, when she came to look back on it, it was as if she had been watching a character in some art house film. And then they were walking through the empty streets of the city, which was very art house as well, and a thin rain was starting. The red headed man in his suit that was dusty and creased, as though he had slept in it one too many nights, pulled on the very end of his cigarette like a drowning man sucking in air and said 'oh shit.' She said that she would have to go because the nuns locked the doors of the hostel before midnight. The friend of a friend said – as if the idea had just occurred to him – 'maybe we could hire a car between us or borrow one and you could drive us down to Cork.'

Taken aback, she said 'But I can't drive. I haven't learnt yet.'

The red headed man, with his bruised face, who had suddenly bent double because the deep breathing seemed to have hurt his ribs, stood upright again and pulled off his glasses, and she could see that he had two black eyes, all bruised and raw with the whites shot through with red veins. He put out his hand and took hold of her arm, and stared at her, really stared at her. She felt a frisson of something that might have been fear or pity or something else altogether.

How old *are* you? he asked.

'I'm eighteen,' she said and he said 'Sweet fucking Jesus Christ almighty! I thought you were twenty five at least.' He looked at his friend and said 'What is she *doing* here? What the fuck is she *doing* here?'

The friend shrugged. She realised that she was very frightened. There was a pause, a space of a few seconds, then the red headed man sighed and shook his head. He took her gently by the shoulders.

'Listen to me. Go home now. This is not for you,' he said.

He turned and walked off down the empty street. He seemed very angry all of a sudden. They followed him, the friend of a friend remonstrating with him. She trailed after them feeling faintly embarrassed, and they walked until they were back on Grafton Street.

'You know your way from here?' asked the friend of a friend.

'Yes but what about him?'

'He'll be fine. Won't you Liam?'

The red headed man turned towards her but he had put his sunglasses back on again and she couldn't see his eyes. His smile was a grimace.

'Oh yes' he said. 'I'll be as right as rain. You go home now, sweetheart. Go home.'

She went back to the hostel. She was almost late. A tight lipped nun was waiting in the hall, rattling a bunch of keys. There was a marble font of holy water to one side of the door.

'Goodnight, sister.' she said.

She dipped her hand into the water, crossed herself, and went up to bed.

Letter From Warsaw 1981

My dear friends, I have been thinking about you and wondering if you were worried about us. Well, it isn't good, but it's better than it was, politically. Economically it is bad, but it was bad before. Now at least we know all about it.

You must have heard and read more about Poland recently than at any time during the last thirty years though I doubt if you can fully realise what is going on here. For the last half year we have lived with enormous uncertainty. We are all engaged with the new trade union, Solidarity. It keeps us very busy and I never suspected that meetings lasting many hours could be so interesting, that the time could pass so quickly.

You know, although I am a Polish woman, I have never concerned myself much with the majority of my compatriots. That we are brave, I already knew. Now I am convinced that we are a splendid nation! People are being kind to each other, disciplined and sensible. They seem to be putting the interests of the country, the region and even the factory first. We were not so kind to each other before. We did not care. But still, deep inside us, there lurked some germ, some fossil of our old selves and it made us at once a cynical and a romantic people. It was as if our true selves had been imprisoned for many years. Trapped, like those delicate little fossils inside the chunks of yellow amber I sometimes work with.

You know that as a silversmith, I have been living and working in Warszawa for some time now. I am, I suppose, known in my field, good at my work. I have even had one or two official commissions and that, for someone who has resisted all invitations to party membership, is indeed an achievement. Oh, the invitations have come. Once when I was working for Stokowski the jeweller he told me, 'Be realistic Lilia. You must be realistic about these things. It will bring you twice as much work, twice as many commissions.' Well, I refused. And once, much later, there was a second invitation from the official who commissioned a silver water set as a gift for some visiting Western dignitary. 'Why don't you join us?' he said. 'Join the party.' One cannot join, you know, except by invitation, so it was a significant request. He was a handsome man with hard, knowing eyes. I expect he was a realist too. 'You would get much more work, you know,' he said.

'But I have enough work,' I told him. And I remember that he made a scornful little sound, pursing his lips together, frowning.

'Real work. Real money. You could be well off, with your talent. You should use it.'

But I shook my head politely and nothing came of those offers or my refusals. Nothing good, but nothing bad either, which was a mercy. If you can picture the misery of the young girl with buck teeth and pigtails whose well-loved father died in Siberia all those years ago, you will understand that I did not have any real temptation to join the party.

Mother is still in the country. She is lucky that, at her age, she does not realise the seriousness of the situation, as Adam likes to call it. She is far from all sources of unrest, isolated from the recent happenings, although provisions are scarce there. I try to take her what I can, when I can: food, soap powder, shampoo, toilet paper. 'That is an unnecessary luxury, Lilka' she tells me. 'We did without before and we can do without now.'

But it is much more comfortable with, Mamusia!' I tell her.

Adam has come to live with me. He and his wife are in the process of getting a divorce. I am very fond of him, but I think I do not love him. He is so young. He lives with me only because housing is such that he cannot find anywhere else to stay until his divorce comes through and even after. Hannah, his wife, has taken a lover but there is no acrimony between her and Adam. In fact she visits us both here. It is a small flat this, even smaller now that Adam has moved his books and some of his other possessions in. We are high above the city, down a long corridor that always has the same mingled but not unpleasant scents of sauerkraut, cigarette smoke and floor polish. Adam finds it more pleasant to share this small space with me than to share his four roomed apartment with his wife. 'She spreads herself everywhere, everywhere!' he says to me. I find this difficult to believe since Hannah is a small and fragile woman and I am tall as well as clumsy, but he affirms that it is true. I am clumsy with everything that is not to do with silver and my work. I have my studio in Mokotow now, further out of the city and there, everything is tranquil, but here it is a different matter. Between my domestic implements and myself, there is a continual war. I do my best to smash them; they try their utmost to cut and bruise and burn me. Adam says that this is not what he means and does not mind it, although he is a tidy man by nature and I wonder how long this harmony between us will last. It is perhaps a political alliance, one of convenience for both of us.

Nevertheless, I am proving quite a good housewife. In autumn, I made jams and jellies and preserved fruits. Adam bought potatoes and we get eggs from his brother in the country, so we are quite well provided. The worst problem is meat. This is rationed, but even the amounts available to us are meagre. Each country has its gastronomic peculiarity, I suppose. Poles have always eaten a lot of meat, perhaps too much, which is why it is difficult for us now, especially since there is very little fish and less cheese. But with summer coming again, we'll have fresh fruit and vegetables.

Economically, we have reached the very bottom and this cannot have happened suddenly, although its effect on us, the consumers, was rapid. Quite simply, during the last thirty years, we have senselessly expanded industry at the expense of agriculture. So we have a lot of problems. One cannot say that there is intransigent poverty for most, but there *is* insufficiency: too little of everything. We must wait, we must queue, constantly. But we must be optimistic too. Besides, we are healthy and don't always care to queue for butter and sweets and such delicacies. With our wartime and post war experiences, we know how to look after ourselves and how to do without things that – for others – are indispensable.

You know, in a few days time, I shall be fifty years old, but for most of my life, I have never realised the strength of the bond holding us all together in this far from happy little piece of land. I thought that I was a member of an elite group of intellectuals, a hermetically sealed group, not interested in those outside, the labourers, the farmworkers. And in the same way, my own group was foreign to those others. We were their 'outsiders'.

My friends were naturally artistic. There was Jurek, the theatre director, with his experimental plays, thinly disguised political protests that nevertheless attracted no more official attention than if they had been state sponsored propaganda. Perhaps they knew that the measure of the group's influence was the breadth of their audience, and that was narrow indeed. Then there was Joanna, designing posters, strange, surrealistic designs that were also a form of manic protest, but so hidden under layers of artistic metaphor and allusion that none but the most finely tuned minds could sense anything but a vague unease about them. Halina was a photographer, travelling about the country, cataloguing ancient monuments, usually churches, for a muscum, but she had her own problems. Her life was full of dreadful mountains and abysses of love and rejection and she was always so engrossed in her own emotional turmoils that the outside world only thinly penetrated her consciousness.

I was fond of them all. We met often, these and others: writers, painters, potters, craftsmen and women working on the reconstruction of the old buildings in the city. Our flats were small and comfortable with a few well chosen antiques bought from the expensive Desa shops, which specialise in such things. Our parties were civilised. We drank tea and vodka together and in the summer, we went to the countryside to gather mushrooms and fruits, make preserves, work on the land without really knowing anything of its hardships. Not like our forebears.

I find myself writing all this in the past, although none of it has yet ended, seemingly, for we still do these things, still meet and drink vodka in our comfortable flats, but nevertheless, everything has changed, has shifted into a different perspective. Our topics of conversation are quite different. Nothing is the same as it was, nor will be again.

I will tell you a story, an incident that happened to me last year. I was in one of the bigger stores on Marszalkowska. It was early spring and still cold outside. The store was full, as usual, not of goods, but of people. Even then, things were not easy here. To buy fresh meat, one had to queue, getting up early in the morning. Distribution was odd. All the grapefruit in Poland, for instance, might turn up in Krakow, or there might be a sudden glut of bananas in Lodz although none were to be found elsewhere. Goods like sugar, tea, coffee, butter might disappear mysteriously from supermarket shelves, to reappear days or weeks later. It is like that here and has been for years. If you see something you need, you try to buy it immediately for it will surely not be there when you return. If you see a queue, you join it, speculatively. The shop was crowded, full of hurrying, angry people and I was hurrying too, when I saw the old man. He seemed to be a vagabond, a tramp, Vladimir or Estragon. His face was ashy grey, a haze of stubble about cheek and chin, his clothes were dirty and ragged and he was staggering about making small groaning noises. He had a friend with him, a younger man, cleaner, less haggard and the friend was pulling at the older man's arm, trying to get him to come away, to stop making an exhibition of himself.

People separated around them. Everybody thought that he was drunk. I did too. Then, suddenly, in the little space left free to him, close to a counter selling flannel nightdresses and pyjamas, he swung around and fell face down on the floor with a soft thump. His companion stepped back, abandoning him, moving away into the crowd. But a well dressed woman, in a smart suit and thin heeled shoes, rushed forward and turned him over. There was a small puddle of urine on the dirty tiled floor and where his face had lain, a little smear of blood. He flopped there, like some macabre doll, face up, eyes closed, his skin a livid grey green colour. The woman stepped back, hand to mouth, looking for help. From the middle of the crowd, I looked up and saw that a policeman was standing on the steps to one of the exits, staring down at us. Then he turned and walked away, very quickly.

I went home, shaking, convinced that the old man had been dead. When I got to the flat, I started to cry and in spite of vodka and warmth, shivered and wept for a long time. The shock seemed out of all proportion to the incident. It gave me nightmares full of pity and desperation for weeks after.

You know, when you work in amber, as you polish it, a fine dust flies up all around you and fills the air with the sweet scent of long dead pine forests. You polish the yellow chunks of it and below the surface, you can see the little fossilised leaves and seeds and insects. Oh we were in amber but it was as if that one event had weakened my golden prison. Soon it would shatter completely.

During the last six months, that seems to have happened. I went to Gdansk for the unveiling of the monument to those who were killed there in 1970, and then on to Gdynia. It was important to me, that visit. I shall remember it all my life, whatever becomes of us. I have never seen so many people together in the same place, so many different sorts of people, so full of emotion, so full of integrity.

My dear friends, this letter is untidy, perhaps because I have tried to write too much and too clearly in a language which is not my own. Nothing is simple but now I shall try to say it all in a few sentences. We are rich in experience. You know, problems are our speciality. Our young people are splendid. We are all of us very tired, although we continue to be sensible and disciplined. But we have determination and it is possible that a situation may arise in which, irrespective of the consequences, we shall have to act against our better judgement. In the name of higher ideals and right. Lilia.

Sardine Burial

Anita and Marianne had a double room on the third floor of the hotel with a balcony overlooking the sea. You could look down into the bay with its anchored yachts, yellow pedalos meandering among them, red and blue fishing boats tied up along the quay. It was February and the sun was shining. They had two weeks 'to get a man each,' said Anita, with a grin. She was an old hand at this, had booked herself a spray tan before they left. 'Tenerife's great. I'll make sure you have a good time.'

Marianne hadn't planned any of it. Anita's best friend had let her down at the last minute. And Marianne's partner of three years had walked out on her a couple of months before. 'I'm very sorry but I've met someone else,' he had said, quite casually. So casually, in fact, that she thought at first she must have misheard him. 'I'm afraid I don't love you any more. I've met someone else.' Then he had packed his bags and left. Her flat, comfortable as it was, seemed very empty without him, though Marianna surprised herself by her lack of real sadness. Perhaps I didn't love him after all, she thought. Perhaps we were just too familiar.

Anita worked in an advertising agency. She was big and sexy, a good natured girl. She and Marianne might never have met but for the fact that they started going to the same evening classes in Spanish Conversation. It was odd for Marianne, this class, because she herself taught English to foreigners at a language school; odd to be on the receiving end of all the methods with which she was so familiar. She spoke French and German but not Spanish. Marianne was a patient teacher. She liked the constant procession of foreigners who came in and out of her classroom, the voluble Italians, the thoughtful Finns, the edgy Slavs. She didn't approve of stereotypes, but where language classes were concerned, national differences mattered, had to be taken into account, the shy coaxed into speech, the naturally garrulous controlled a little so that everyone could benefit.

Although she was not yet thirty, she worried that she was growing dull, set in her ways. At the evening class, Marianne and Anita sat next to each other and then started going for a drink together afterwards. Anita was learning Spanish because of Tenerife. 'I've been three times now and I can only ask for a beer or a *cuba libre*,' she said, downing her third rum and coke. Anita's vitality and exuberance attracted Marianne. She even found herself imitating her friend's way of dressing.

For three days, they lay on the beach. Anita, not a natural blonde, soon went brown, but Marianne turned beetroot and burned. Anita lay there, topless and voluptuous, while Marianne sat under an umbrella, fully clothed, or wallowed in the sea to cool off. The hotel pool was icy cold but the sea was warm and the beach golden. 'They imported it from the Sahara, you know,' remarked Anita. Each day, the sand was sifted by a machine to keep it clean for the tourists. By day, the smell of coconut oil hung over it in a fragrant cloud. By night, stray dogs and beach bums slept on it.

On their fourth day, Marianne got bored with the beach. She left Anita grilling gently and went for a walk through the town, all by herself. She gazed at tee-shirts, sarongs, key rings with small bunches of plastic bananas dangling from them and intricate drawn thread linen tablecloths, but she bought nothing. When she returned to the beach, it was to find Anita sitting up, talking to two young Englishmen. One was tanned, fit and good looking, like Anita. The other was beetroot red and peeling. Hard to tell what he looked like under all that sunburn and calamine lotion.

Anita smiled up at her. 'Marianne, this is Colin and this is – '

'Derek,' the young man said. His eyes slid away from Marianne's face in embarrassment. Oh God, this one's mine, I suppose. She could almost hear him thinking it.

They went for a drink to one of the cafes in the tiled piazza. Afterwards, she remembered thinking that their waiter had nice eyes. He smiled at them all impartially as he gave them their drinks. It was his job to smile, to be kind to the tourists, but he smiled with his eyes too. When Colin, trying to order another round, whistled to him like a dog, she frowned, wanting to protest. But she said nothing, afraid of upsetting the congeniality of the party. And afterwards she was ashamed of herself. Ashamed of her companions.

Later on, they went to a different restaurant for paella, and then Anita and Colin went back to their hotel room while Derek and Marianne walked along the seashore. They talked about the sunshine and the weather in Britain, but they didn't so much as hold hands. Anita had suggested, said Derek, that they might like to make up a foursome and share a hire car to see the volcano.

'Good idea,' said Marianne, miserably. Why am I here, she thought. What am I doing here? After a decent interval had elapsed, Derek walked her back to the hotel. Colin was waiting in the bar. 'Anita's in bed,' he said, with a self satisfied smile. He bought her and Derek a drink and then the two men left. She heard them laughing together before they were out of the door.

At the end of their first week, Anita took an unwise dip in the sea, swallowed some water and spent most of the night in their lavatory, groaning. In the morning, she was running a high temperature and in some pain. A doctor was called. He diagnosed gastro enteritis and sent her to bed for a couple of days. Marianne collected five different kinds of medicine from the *Farmacia*, with written instructions, translated into English, on how they were to be administered. Colin called but hearing about Anita's illness left messages of sympathy and then went to the beach. Marianne saw him there later with Derek, talking to a group of French girls. In the evening, when Anita was sleeping, Marianne went out again, alone.

It was Carnival week in Los Cristianos and there was a big fairground at the top end of the town with dodgems, roundabouts and stalls selling beer in paper cups, almond cakes and doughnuts. She wandered around, exhilarated by the crowds. Although the town itself was always full of tourists, here at the fairground, the Canarians seemed to have congregated. The language was much quicker and more breathy than she would ever have suspected from her few rather pedestrian lessons in mainland Spanish. She took pleasure in simply listening to the unfamiliar sounds.

One of the stalls, more vivid than most, attracted her attention. There was a crowd gathered around it. Pushing her way to the front, she saw that it was a Camel Race. A dozen or so brightly coloured model camels with little riders were set on an illuminated track, high up on the stall. Below, were sloping wooden frames. The stallholder pushed a button to start the race and a dozen competitors threw balls up each frame, trying to make them fall through one of eight or so holes punched in the wood. Depending on each person's skill, his or her chosen camel moved forward. She spent a euro learning how to do it and then had another go. A bell rang loudly and to her amazement the boy leaned over and handed her a brightly coloured carnival doll.

The doll had a rag body and a big plastic head with a shock of pink woolly hair. Its face was painted with smiling clown's features and it wore a blue, white and yellow suit. Someone patted her on the back. '*Chochona*,' said a chorus of voices around her.

'What?' she asked, confused.

They pointed to the doll. '*Chochona! Chochona!*'

She was enchanted by the doll. She had never won anything quite so big, so bold and bright. She clutched it close and walked off through the fairground in a happy daze. Her only regret was that she had nobody to share the moment with. Anita, screaming with laughter, bubbling over with enthusiasm, would have been welcome. Presently, she found herself down at the piazza, outside their usual cafe. The waiter came up to her table. He patted the doll's pink woolly head and laughed aloud.

'*Y viva la chochona, para la campeona,*' he chanted. It was what they had said at the stall. Long live the chochona for the champion. 'You win this yourself?' he asked.

She nodded.

'Good for you. What can I get you?'

She tried out her careful Spanish on him. '*Naranja, por favor.*'

'Narang-ha.' He mocked her gently. His good humour was irrepressible. 'Ok. Orange.' Then he frowned suddenly, looking around. He was looking for Anita. 'Are you all alone?' he asked.

'My friend is sick.' She patted her stomach. He nodded sympathetically. 'It happens. Mostly to visitors. We get used to our own bugs!'

She noticed his nice brown forearms and his very white shirt with the sleeves rolled up. He had very white teeth too. He was a little younger than she was, perhaps twenty five or so. He went away and came back with a laden tray, holding it high, carrying several orders at once. He looked as though he enjoyed his work, always smiling at people, joking with them in a variety of languages. He kept her orange juice till last and put it down in front of her with a flourish. '*Senorita.*' Then he frowned again. 'Is your friend very sick?' he asked.

'She must stay in bed for two days,' she replied, lapsing into her correct language teacher's English.

'It's OK,' he said, laughing again. 'I understand you. But you? You have friends here?'

'No. No friends. But I'll be fine. I'll go to the beach. Maybe go on a coach trip round the island. There's plenty to do.'

He went away but a little while later he was back again. 'I've fixed it.' She felt mildly alarmed. What had he fixed? 'Tomorrow, I work till three. Then I have free time till seven. I have to work again at seven. I can borrow a car from my friend. Take you for a drive. To see – ' He hesitated. '*Almendras.* Very beautiful. You know what this is?'

She knew. Almonds. The almond trees on the lower slopes of the mountains were in full bloom. She hesitated. Afraid of what? She wanted to go. She liked him. He exuded a kind of natural courtesy. He saw her hesitation. 'It's OK. I'm a good man. Do you understand? No funny business!'

She grinned at him. 'I understand. No funny business.'

It occurred to her that she might not be averse to a little funny business, but still, his openness was refreshing.

'My name is Luis,' he said. 'And you?'

'Marianne.'

'Marianna. Good. I'll meet you here tomorrow.' He went back to work, whistling.

The car was a clapped out Fiat with a slipping clutch but Luis drove well and – she was pleased to note – courteously. They drove out of town, past the acres of new building, and then they were climbing slowly towards the mountains. The arid lower slopes and valleys were softened by a haze of pale pink and white almond blossom, delicate and ephemeral after the blousy poinsettias and hibiscus of the town. She had never seen such a wealth of blossom, not even on English hawthorn hedges in May, when she was a little girl.

'Look at it. Just look at it,' she kept saying.

He seemed gratified by her admiration, taking it as a compliment to his home. Presently, they left the blossoming slopes behind and were driving through the silent Canary pine forests.

When he stopped the car and they got out, she noticed that the air had a little freshness to it, a little intimation of the snows that still covered the slopes of Teide, high above the clouds.

'We have a picnic,' he said proudly, producing a bag with slices of cold tortilla, buttered rolls, small sweet bananas and bottled beer. They sat on a blanket on the ground, ate and drank. The food tasted wonderful. Two small, unknown birds twittered from the treetops. The land sloped away, rocky and inhospitable, but plants clung to the patchy soil and the ground was littered with oversized pine cones. After their meal, she rushed about, collecting cones. He watched her, at first amused by her enthusiasm at something so commonplace, but then he joined in, hunting out the biggest and the best. They filled the picnic bag, cramming them in. Occasionally, a car passed them on its way down the mountain but otherwise they were undisturbed. The sun was setting over the sea as they drove back to town. The sky was clear and they saw the humped shapes of the islands of La Gomera and Hierro in the distance.

'You'll be late for work,' she said.

'No problem. They owe me some time. But I have no car tomorrow. Will you come for a walk with me?'

'Yes. Why not? I'd love to come for a walk with you.'

The following day, Anita was feeling well enough to sit out on their balcony

'Oh my God,' she said, when her friend came in. 'Not a Spanish waiter, Marianne.'

'Why not?'

'It's just such a cliché, isn't it?'

Later that night, when Luis had finished his shift, he took Marianne to a German bar. It had red roses on the tables, a tiny dance floor. She had become physically very aware of him. He was a kind man. An attractive man. They drank, talked and danced until the bar closed at three. He held her very close and as they left, the proprietor gave her one of the roses. Luis walked her back to the hotel. On the way there, they sat on the wall above the beach and he kissed her. Through the thin silk of her dress, she could feel his heart beating against her breast.

He told her a little about himself. He had been in England for six months, working as waiter, but he had been desperately homesick and he couldn't stand the weather. When winter came, and as soon as he could get his air fare together, he had flown home.

'To Los Cristianos?' she asked.

'Ah no. Not Los Cristianos.' He paused, hesitating. 'I'm going home tomorrow. Just for a day. I have a day off. Do you want to come?'

'Where's home then?'

He pointed out into the bay. 'La Gomera. You saw it yesterday. The island over there. It is very beautiful. Will you come?'

But the next morning, Anita was feeling much better. She had made plans for the day. Marianne had upset them. 'You're surely not going to La Gomera with a waiter are you?' she exclaimed in disgust. 'Not when we've hired a car to go up Teide.'

'Who has?'

'Colin and Derek and the two of us.'

'Well, I'm sorry, but I'm going to La Gomera with Luis. I've promised.'

Anita had never known her friend to be so firm. It was most uncharacteristic.

'But that means Derek will have to play gooseberry,' she said, plaintively. 'And I wanted to spend the day with Colin.'

'I don't even like Derek. I'm sorry, but I'm not going to get saddled with him just because you want Colin all to yourself. I don't see why they have to go around in a twosome anyway. Why can't Derek find his own girlfriend?'

Anita knew when she was beaten and friendly relations were

resumed. She was never one to bear a grudge but contented herself with saying, a little vindictively, 'You really must have got it bad for this *waiter*.'

The ferry ate up the miles between the two islands. Gomera had steep sides and jagged cliffs with banana plantations in the valleys. 'It's very green, inland,' said Luis. 'One day, maybe, we can get a car and I can show you all of it. It is very beautiful, my home. We had a terrible fire some years ago, but things are growing again.'

She didn't think there would be enough time for her to come back again, let alone get a car, but she didn't say so.

It was around ten o'clock when the ferry docked at San Sebastian, the capital of the island. There were cactus trees in the square. They drank coffee outside a bar where everyone seemed to know Luis. Men and women greeted him, asked him questions, smiled and waved at him. There were curious but not unfriendly stares for her. Once or twice, he introduced her as 'My friend from England. She teaches English.' They would think she was someone he had met in London, not someone he had picked up in a cafe in Los Cristianos. She wondered if that was his intention.

San Sebastian was a curious mixture of beauty and ugliness. There were mediaeval shuttered buildings with tantalising glimpses of green courtyards beyond half open doors. Higher up the hillside were new buildings, unfinished houses and half dug plots. Occasionally there was a thin dog tied to a chain, guarding heaven knew what. She wondered why so few of the houses had real windows. And those that had were heavily shuttered. 'It is cool in summer,' Luis told her when she asked him. 'Besides – ' he shot her a sidelong glance. 'We live in caves here. Once upon a time.'

Once, she looked up and caught a glimpse of a head peering out of a casement in one of the shutters. An old woman looked down, pale and toothless, with a black scarf wound around her head. Then, as though alarmed by so much sunlight, the head was suddenly withdrawn and the casement quickly pulled shut.

'When are we going to your house?' she asked.

'Soon,' he said. 'Soon.'

He took her to the ancient church with its carved and painted wooden altars. Inside, in the cool gloom, she felt naked and out of place. She was wearing shorts and a tee-shirt but he seemed unaware of her embarrassment. Columbus had left from this port on his voyage to the Indies, but not before he had had an affair with a local princess, Beatriz de Bobadilla. Luis told her all about it in a whisper, laughing about it.

In fourteen hundred and ninety two, Columbus sailed the ocean blue, she thought. On one of the walls was the remains of a fresco with galleons, their sails and flags flying, and the towers of a town, perhaps San Sebastian itself, just visible in the foreground.

'Are those Columbus's ships?' she asked.

'I don't know. I don't think so. I think this is much later.'

'How can you live here and not know?'

He smiled. 'Only tourists know things like that. We just live here.'

They had lunch, sandwiches and cool beers, outside another bar. Then they climbed the hill above the town to where a tall, white statue of Christ stood on a concrete pillar, blessing the harbour and the sea. He had a halo of light bulbs about his head and offerings of flowers and candles at his feet, but his fingers were broken. From the hill top they could see Teide, floating on a sea of cloud above the rest of Tenerife. Holding up the sky, she thought. She wondered if Anita and Colin were enjoying themselves up there and if Derek had gone too. It was windy on the hillside and bleak. Tiny baby bushes that had seeded themselves in profusion were scattered across the slopes among the fleshy prickly pears. She shivered in the wind. He pulled her close, kissed her. He had a thin, hard body. Then he sat up and looked out to sea with one arm around her.

'Marianna, Marianna,' he said as though savouring the name.

At last, he stood up. 'Come on,' he said. 'We must go to my house.'

It was already past three o'clock. The ferry back to Los Cristianos left at five thirty. Not much time, she thought. They got a lift down the hill road in a tourist bus full of elderly German ladies. She sat in the only available seat and Luis stood and conversed in rapid Spanish with the driver whom he seemed to know well. An old school friend, he said.

Once in the town they crossed the main square and then walked up the hill again, along narrow lanes and up flights of stone stairs. He went ahead at a great pace until she was breathless and dizzy in the heat.

'Slow down,' she pleaded.

He looked back, contrite. 'I'm sorry. We'll rest a minute.'

Why had he left it so late? Why was he in such a hurry now?

'Are you angry about something?' she asked.

'No, no. I'm not angry.' He squeezed her hand. As they came up to a neat villa with a red tiled roof, she thought they had arrived. A middle aged woman was watering a well kept garden. She smiled and spoke to Luis. Marianne prepared herself for introductions but after a quick word, Luis moved on.

'I thought that was your house,' she said.

He shook his head firmly. 'No. Not that one.'

They set off again, past a scruffy minimarket, past a corner bar. Then they were out of town on a track that lead through scrubby fields. An old fashioned windmill raised a salute against the sky. Two goats thrust their hooves over a wall at Luis's approach and he greeted them like old friends, patting their heads. A donkey peered over an earth bank. She saw a pig in a sty of stones. Closer, there was another building, part of the hillside itself. Like a cave, she thought. Perhaps it was some sort of stable. Then, she realised that it was a house.

Afterwards, when she tried to remember it, it was all very vague. The house was spotlessly clean and smelled of bleach but it was very hard to make out many details in the sudden darkness, after the sunlight outside. She remembered an all-purpose living room with a cooker and sink, a Formica table and three brown easy chairs. A chest of drawers, crammed with family photographs, stood against one wall. The walls themselves were hung with pictures, the Virgin of Candelaria, a gory Christ on the cross, a curiously anatomical Sacred Heart. A set of wooden rosary beads hung from a nail. There were two curtained doorways, beyond which she guessed must be the bedrooms. The poverty stunned her. She could only think of her nice flat, the light rooms, the comfort of it. Later, she remembered an elderly woman dressed all in black. She had a toothless grin, like the face at the casement. A younger woman with a thin, tired face came forward to greet her. She must be Luis's mother. She had his beautiful eyes. Two young children, Marie Carmen and Eduardo, were eating bread and jam at the table. Marie Carmen got up and hugged her brother, chatting to him in a flood of quick, excited Spanish. Two small brown dogs chased their tails, and each other, round and round the room for pure joy until they were shooed out of doors.

Marianne lost count of the size of his family. She felt bemused. Where did they all sleep? Then, his father came in, embraced his son. He had a round belly and white teeth in a sunburnt face. He was like a bigger, more worn version of his son. Like an old statue with the surfaces all rubbed and damaged, she thought. His hands were calloused and hard. When he shook hands with her, he crushed her fingers, but it wasn't deliberate.

She was given coffee and cake which she ate in silence. They spoke no English and Luis did not offer to translate. She smiled at them till her face ached and they flocked around Luis like starlings. Plainly they all adored him.

'What are they saying?' she asked.

'Nothing. No matter,' he said. 'No matter.'

She was relieved when it was time to go.

Going back on the ferry, Luis sat silently beside her. 'The people who live on La Gomera, on all these islands, some of them once lived in caves,' he ventured, after a while. 'Not now. They don't live in caves. Not really. But there is no shame in poverty.'

'Oh, but I didn't think – I mean – ' she was suddenly floundering. What did she mean? She stopped. In denying it, the admission was made. He put his hand over hers. 'It is very poor. They are very poor. I know. But it is their home. They are proud of it. I am proud of them.' He was making a great effort with his English.

Later she read that the Gomerans had once communicated with each other across the steep-sided valleys of their island by whistling. He too was whistling across the abyss that had suddenly opened between them, but the words were strange to her. She could hardly grasp their meaning.

'I only have a little money,' he said. 'There is nothing I can do. Anyway, they do not want anything. It is home.' There was a pause. She said nothing, not knowing what to say. Whatever she said would sound wrong, patronising. Perhaps that was the measure of the difference between them. He stared at the sea, his shoulders hunched dejectedly. After a while, she felt cold in the evening wind and went inside to sit down, but it was a long time before he joined her.

'Did you have a good day?' asked Anita, back at the hotel. Derek had found himself a girl. Teide had been wonderful.

'Yes, thank-you. It was a lovely day. A beautiful island.' But they had made no arrangement to meet again.

On Saturday night, Carnival ended. Anita, the two men and

the other girl, whose name was Susie, went to watch the Burial of the Sardine, the traditional end to the festivities and Marianne went with them. Susie was plainly infatuated with Derek. His sunburn had mellowed and Marianne noticed that he was quite good looking after all.

A large model sardine, constructed of wood and paper, was carried on a bier through the streets of the town. Behind, in procession, came a crowd of townspeople, mostly young, all dressed in black. The men were dressed up as old women, in black dresses, stockings, shoes, cardigans and veils. They loudly bewailed the death of the sardine and the end of carnival. They mourned and wept all over unsuspecting tourists. In spite of herself, she laughed. With great ceremony, they carried the fish down to the beach and burned it in a flurry of firecrackers and rockets. Soon, there was nothing left but a few charred pieces of wood.

It was all great fun but underneath it, amid the noise and light, she sensed something older and much more primitive at work, sensed it and was half excited by it, half afraid of it. Pagan misrule. A dangerous suspension of normality. Afterwards, they went to the cafe where Luis worked. She had never told Anita which one he worked in and now she didn't dare to protest. He ignored them, sending another waiter to their outside table. After a while, she got up under the pretence of going to the ladies and went inside to speak to him. He was waiting at the bar with a tray half full of drinks.

'What have I done?' she asked. 'That's all I want to know. What did I do wrong?'

When he turned to look at her, she saw his face so full of love and sadness that she found herself trembling. 'Nothing,' he said. 'You have done nothing, Marianna. But you know as well as I do what is the matter. Perhaps I should not have taken you to my home, but then it would have been a lie. As it is, I saw the fear on your face. You suspected me of something wrong.' He hesitated. 'Of perhaps wanting something from you. I wanted nothing. They are only ordinary people. I love them.'

What could she say? Fear? Yes. She had been a little afraid. Wouldn't anybody in her position have been afraid?

'Disgust at such poverty I might have overcome,' he continued. He was choosing his words carefully as though he had thought deeply about them. Perhaps he had. 'But fear? I thought you might be different. You loved the *almendras*. When I saw you gathering the pine cones, I thought – ' He stopped again. 'But then I saw your smiling face full of fear. Fear is hard. They are good people. I am a good man.'

She didn't doubt it. A good man is hard to find. The sentence came floating into her head. She had used it often enough in her lessons to amuse her students. Now it returned to mock her.

'But I'm going home on Tuesday,' she said, in a panic.

He filled his tray with more glasses, gin and tonic, rum and coke.

'A pity,' he said. 'Maybe you write to me here. Maybe you help my English, eh?' He took her hand and squeezed it briefly. 'You write to me here. You come back when you are truly not afraid. Then maybe I take you to my home again.'

She went back to their table.

'What became of your Spanish waiter?' asked Anita, maliciously. Had she seen or had it merely been a shot in the dark?

Marianne forced a smile. She looked from Anita to Colin. Colin's eyes were already straying to other tables, other girls. But then Anita wouldn't care.

'You know what holiday romances are,' Marianne said. 'They last about as long as – ' She glanced down to the beach, 'As that poor old sardine down there. But at least they gave him a decent send-off.'

She drank her wine and ordered another glass. Perhaps next

year, she would come back. Perhaps she would be a little less afraid. But how did one become brave, open to experience?

A good man is hard to find.

Beside their table, exotic purple and orange hibiscus flowers had unfurled themselves in the day's sunshine. Now they drooped a little. Soon they would fold and crumple like tissue paper. They glowed with a curious radiance in the failing light. Never mind, she thought. Maybe next year. Anything, after all, was possible.

The Sampler

Susan saw the sampler in the catalogue before she saw it in reality. 'A mid nineteenth century needlework sampler by Janet Harvey, in memory of Thomas Harvey, who died on the 19th of March, 1845.' She had pulled a face at the subject matter, although she had a fondness for samplers that looked good on the plain walls of their cottage sitting room. She dealt in antique textiles in a small way, buying at auction and occasionally at boot sales, selling online or from a stall at a local antique market. Samplers always went well, and she liked them so much that she didn't mind living with them for a while. She wondered if this one had perhaps been made by a widow as a memorial to her husband. There was no picture in the catalogue so perhaps it had been a late entry. On viewing day she began to hunt around the saleroom for the appropriate lot number.

She found it hanging in a shaft of dusty sunlight, between two oil paintings of highland cattle. It was lunchtime and the saleroom was quiet. The dealers had all gone off to the cafe down the road to eat overpriced sandwiches, drink oversized mugs of coffee and figure out how high they were prepared to go on this or that item.

She leaned forward to read the little black letters stitched so precisely onto the canvas.

In memory of Thomas Harvey, my son, who died aged 5 months on the 19th day of March, 1845.

'Oh!' she said, aloud. She hadn't thought it might be a child. But why not? Infancy was a dangerous time back then. Beneath the sad statement of dedication was a four line rhyme. She could just make it out, although the brown silk had faded somewhat. Browns often faded to cream on these old samplers, making it hard to decipher names and dates.

They who life's longest lease enjoy
Have told us with a sigh
That to be born seems little more
Than to begin to die.

How grim. How typical. Poor little Thomas hadn't enjoyed life's longest lease though, had he?

Rather surprisingly for a mourning sampler, the rest of the stitches were worked in coloured silks. Stylized trees and flowers surrounded and belied the inscription and the stern verse. They were intricate and very pretty and she could see that their colours must once have been strong and warm. There was a strawberry border with linked fruits, there were tall tulips and daffodils, a bird, a small gambolling dog. For some reason, the dog touched her. She imagined it sitting beside Janet, keeping her company as she stitched. Had she wept as she stitched? Of course she had. Why did people think that the Victorians found the deaths of their loved ones any less devastating, just because they were commonplace?

As she read through the inscription a second time, she became uncomfortably aware of the power of the emotion behind it. Her own body responded to it. It seemed to radiate passionately from the canvas and hold her for an instant, flooding every part of her, dazzling her with love rather than grief, love *and* grief perhaps. She swayed back, feeling a lump rising in her throat and tears prickling behind her eyes. She was embarrassed by the intensity of her own response. Surreptitiously, she fumbled in her pocket for a tissue and blew her nose.

Susan divided her friends and colleagues into three groups: those who had begun early, those who had left it late and those who had never started at all. Children, of course. The offspring of those who had begun early were all grown or nearly grown and these couples were variously embarking on new ways of living, with anticipation or disappointment. Some seemed to be embracing their freedom enthusiastically but she saw others edging suspiciously around their partners. These were couples who had grown apart in a welter of child caring and rearing. Some were managing the transition but others were already divorced. Those who had begun late were still absorbed in all the fascinations of infancy. She supposed that she and her husband, Mike, must belong to the third group: those who had never had any children at all, either through personal choice or through disappointment, in love or fertility. But where had their choices or disappointments been? They had never tried and that was down to her. She knew that Mike didn't really accept their childlessness and perhaps he never would. He didn't seem to want to debate it with her, but he wasn't happy about it either.

They had made no momentous decisions. For years, they had drifted along together very contentedly, indulging in words such as 'when' and 'if' and 'maybe'. Perhaps their contentment had been part of the problem. They were very happy as they were. The longer she put off trying for a baby the more impossible it seemed, the more problems she could foresee. Mike wouldn't pressurize her but she sensed his unspoken disappointment, the suppressed longing as he played with his nieces and nephews, the eagerness with which he would point out their good points. She usually found herself agreeing with him, laughing with him, enjoying the moment. But she had never been naturally maternal or even particularly tolerant with children. Her friends knew it and tried to curb their tendency to talk about their offspring all the time. Susan didn't understand the peculiar combination of indulgence and insult with which they approached their small children.

'Who'd have kids?' Alice would say. Alice was a fellow antique dealer, specializing in handbags and vintage clothes. They had met at a regular antique market and now their stalls were always side by side. Sometimes they would swap items. Susan would find scarves and hankies at the bottom of boxes of linen. Alice would look out for tablecloths, lengths of lace, embroidered pictures. They would do little deals between the two of them, mind each other's stalls while they went to the loo or grabbed a coffee, share sandwiches and cake. Sometimes Alice's husband would come in, carrying Alice's toddler strapped to his back, so that his pudgy fingers were well away from the tantalizing objects on display.

'Oh, it just gets worse and worse!' Alice would say. Then she would sweep her son up into her arms, in spite of the pee soaked trousers which made Susan wince. 'He won't have his nappies on but he keeps forgetting. Johnnie, even your socks are wet! They're revolting. You're revolting, Johnnie!' And then she would kiss him and he would chuckle and duck his head, bashful and delighted at the same time.

'It isn't compulsory,' Susan wanted to say, but held her tongue for the sake of friendship.

Just sometimes, though, the awful vulnerability of the soft place at the back of a child's head, or the sight of a small girl in a too-large sleep suit, padding about on flat white feet, sparked off a sudden involuntary craving that alarmed her with its strength and poignancy. Whenever she held a newborn in her inexperienced arms, the warmth that seemed to be generated by this small powerhouse took her by surprise.

She thought about Janet Harvey and how for her there would have been no choices, no agonising. Either children would have come along or they wouldn't. Their absence would have been more of a disaster than now, when choices were possible, encouraged even. There were initials on the sampler, a little row of them: EH, AH, GH, JH, another AH, DH. Other children? Maybe. Maybe Thomas had been a last late baby. Maybe that had been the problem. Or maybe it had been one of those awful childhood illnesses like diphtheria, tetanus, polio. Who knew? She supposed it would be possible to do some research online, look up Janet and her son Thomas. She liked to research her antiques, enjoyed finding out about them almost more than selling them. Most likely there would be some genealogical index somewhere with those names and that precise date of death for Thomas. She would be able to find out if there had been other children, what their names had been, who had been their father, Janet's husband. One of the AH initials had a little crown over it, and she knew that this might indicate the head of the household: Alan, Andrew, Albert? Samplers like this were gold dust for genealogists, especially where they could help to confirm dates and details when families were large and life was precarious.

If she admitted the truth, Susan knew that she was frightened, frightened of the self surrender and the risk that seemed to be involved in childbearing, the loss of privacy. It seemed a small thing and she was ashamed of herself. But her panic was very real. She was afraid of growing away from her husband, terrified of the messiness of childbirth. Her friends told apocalyptic stories of blood and pain beyond enduring, of dreadful indignities. They seemed to delight in relating these experiences as though they had all happened to somebody else and not themselves.

'You forget,' they said vaguely, when she demanded to know why, if it was all so bad, they had had more children. Another of her friends, Marie, was a mother of four. They had met at a book group, got on instantly, found that they had the same taste in reading, liked each other a lot.

'But you do forget,' Marie asserted again.

'Even after four?'

'Even then. The second is best. I reckon the second is always easiest. Well, that was the way it was with me. Perhaps the fourth too. But you know me. I might have gone for another if Alec hadn't put his foot down.'

'You wouldn't!' Susan was disbelieving. Marie's house was warm, chaotic, and if you arrived in the daytime, it would inevitably be covered in small and mostly anonymous bits of brightly coloured plastic, her hallway piled with shoes of all shapes and sizes, shoes belonging to her children and all their friends.

'Oh I would. Like shelling peas. That's the way it was for me. And I love babies, you know. Love them!'

'Everyone should have at least one child!' Alice had once remarked, thoughtlessly, outrageously really. Susan had bitten her tongue, wanting to challenge her friend but stopping herself just in time.

'Why?' she asked.

'Because it changes you so much!'

'But perhaps I don't want to change. I don't want me and Mike to change at all.'

'You don't know until you try it.'

'Will it make us any happier than we are now?'

'Not happier. Not really.'

'Then what?'

'It isn't happiness. Well, it is. But you worry. You worry all the time. It changes you in ways you never expect. For better and for worse. You find out things about yourself and other people.'

'I used to think I was patient until I had kids. Now I scream at them all the time,' said Marie, ruefully.

'Then why carry on having them? I think it's a plot to make us suffer the way you all do.'

They laughed. They were sitting in the pub, a small group of close women friends. They went to the pub most weeks, after their book group, to chat and drink wine. You could tell who was pregnant by the orange juice.

'Besides,' said Susan, 'What if you have kids and then discover you don't really like them after all? You can't give them back, can you? It isn't like adopting a puppy.'

'Oh, you quite often don't like them,' said Marie. 'You love them all the time, but I find I can't bear my lot sometimes. Endless liking isn't compulsory you know.'

'The problem is,' added Alice, 'That afterwards you're a different person from before. I mean completely different. You can hardly even remember the way you were before. You enter another world. It's a bit like bereavement. That changes your perspective completely too.' Alice had lost her father the year before and was still missing him, still needing to talk about him compulsively. 'It's like joining a club. Both things are. Except that having children is an awful lot nicer!'

'You become vulnerable. That's it,' said Marie. 'Through your children. You were never vulnerable before. You couldn't even imagine being that vulnerable. That's why you try to treat it lightly. Pretend that you don't care. You have a hostage to fortune – or several – and you have to try to distract her. Fortune, I mean. If there is such a thing!'

'After Johnnie was born, I was so ill that for a month I wished him away. I wished every morning and certainly most of the night that I could wake up and he wouldn't be there. I don't mean I wished him to be ill or anything. Just that he had never happened. People are afraid to admit that, you know. In public anyway. You're supposed to bond madly, right away.'

'So why are you admitting it now?' asked Susan. She couldn't imagine it. Not really.

'Because I've had a couple of glasses of wine. Because we *should* admit these things. Then we'd all feel better about ourselves. And besides, I knew I would be quite capable of killing to defend him.

Still would. Then you get to know this little creature and it's like a love affair. You get fed up sometimes but you know that you're never going to get over it even when you're dog tired and he won't go to sleep, or when he's been sick over you for the umpteenth time.'

Susan shook her head. 'Sounds a bit too much like self sacrifice to me.'

'No. You're not sacrificing anything. You do it in the same way that you would bandage your own hand if you cut it. That's the problem. And the joy. There's a lot of joy.'

A little while ago, some small hormonal problem had sent Susan to her doctor and then to a consultant. To her relief, he had run some tests and told her that there was nothing wrong with her. Except that she was thirty eight. She had found herself asking him about pregnancy.

'Well, you're a bit old for a first time,' he had said. 'But not too old. There are disadvantages. And we can't predict fertility you know. Especially after thirty five or so. But there are big advantages too. You don't smoke, you're healthy and sensible. There isn't much risk and we'd look after you. But you can't leave it much longer.' When she looked askance, he had hastened to add, 'I'm not suggesting you have to decide one way or the other, you understand. That's entirely up to you. None of my business. And it's a huge commitment, so you have to be sure you want it. But from a medical point of view, I can advise you that you should make the decision, whatever it is, and make it quite soon. After all, you've never put your fertility to the test yet, have you? You don't know how long it might take.'

Today, she thought about Janet Harvey sewing all her grief for that small life into this linen canvas, hour after hour, day after day, stitch after painful stitch. It was hardly to be borne. She looked at it and again felt herself momentarily possessed by a woman's grief and its submersion in the repetitive habit of needlework, a grief so strong that after a hundred and fifty years it could still reach out and touch her, not darkly but with stark and terrible illumination.

An older woman, another dealer she knew slightly, was peering at the sampler over her shoulder.

Susan whispered, 'A hostage to fortune.'

'Sorry? Did you say something, dear?'

'No. Nothing. Just talking to myself. Remembering something somebody said.'

'Well, it's very pretty. But a gloomy theme all the same, don't you think? I shan't be putting in a bid anyway. Doubt if I could find a buyer for it very quickly, although some collectors will buy anything in their chosen field. I suppose you could put it online and pretend it's haunted.' She laughed.

'Maybe it is!'

The woman recoiled a little. 'Do you think so?'

'Not really. Only by grief. Don't you think?'

'Well, perhaps you're right.'

Susan thought about coming back the next day and making a bid. There was nothing else for her in this sale so it would mean making a special trip. For a while, she toyed with the idea, intrigued by the possibilities for researching the Harvey family. But later, when she sat in the nearby cafe with a big mug of coffee and a granola bar, she thought better of it. She knew that she wouldn't be bidding on this particular item. She suspected the other dealer was right. The sampler wouldn't be a quick sale. It was the kind of thing you would have to live with for some time, looking for the right buyer, the right collector. And it wouldn't do to be habitually at the mercy of an old grief.

Besides, there were other things to think about. She smiled. The coffee was hot and strong and gave her a little kick inside. She had her own risks to take.

A Bad Year For Trees

It had been a bad year for trees. The ash trees in the deer park were the first to go. They were diseased and there was no help for it. Martin mourned them like old friends, stooping over their fallen carcasses and cursing under his breath so that the forestry workers called in to do the felling shouldn't hear him and think him foolish. In late spring, there came freak gales from the wrong direction. The prevailing winds here were westerly and the trees had long ago learned which way they ought to bend. The sudden change, this onslaught from the east, brought many casualties: a tangle of fallen hazel and beech in the plantation that sheltered garden from shore. A wet summer had given them only a small respite, the odd day of sunshine now and then. The relentless downpours had loosened the soil around shallow roots. The inevitable winter winds would wreak havoc again. And now, looking up at the birch grove that divided precise terraces from conifers striding in serrated ranks up the hill above the big house, he saw that the birches there were growing old and could not be expected to last for much longer.

Martin was the head gardener in this small country park where visitors came to walk and picnic each summer. Sometimes the house was open to the public; more often it was just the gardens and a tiny cafe. The owners encouraged plant sales, buying in herbaceous plants and pretending they came from the gardens. But it was already late October and now the gardeners could go about their business in peace. He didn't like summer visitors, seeing them as a necessary evil. They parked their cars where they shouldn't. They stole cuttings, nipping soft stems when they thought nobody was looking and folding them into damp tissue. Old ladies were the worst culprits. Martin always suspected that their handbags were stuffed with their ill gotten gains. If he had his way, he would have searched them on the way out. The youngsters dropped litter, picked flowers and etched their initials into tree trunks. Families brought portable barbecues and lit them on picnic tables, scorching the wood. Earlier that year, he had come across a hedgehog staggering blindly along a gravel path with its head firmly jammed into a can, cutting a ludicrous little figure. Anger rose in him as he caught and freed the terrified animal.

He had moved to a small cottage on this estate some twenty years earlier while his daughter, Rosie, was a baby and his wife was still alive. But his wife had died after a sudden, swift illness, only a few years previously. After her death, his work in the small enclosed world of the park had begun to intrude upon him to an intolerable degree. He saw the growing and dying, the preying of parasitic plant upon plant or bird upon small animal with searing clarity. If so much as a rose tree in the walled garden withered he felt something wither and die in him also. It was as though he had no defences, had shed some protective skin. Last winter he had found birds on the beach, guillemots and razorbills, staggering ashore, their wings black with oil. There had been no official notification of any spillage but sometimes ships would void their tanks out at sea. There was little that could be done for the creatures, although he tried, he and a handful of volunteers, trapping the sickly birds, trying to clean them. But it was the poison they had swallowed that had done most damage and there was little they could do about that. Most of them died. At the time he had raged around the cottage that seemed too small to contain his passion for these vulnerable living things. He frightened his daughter and was sorry for it later. But the tragedies of land and sea ate into him and there seemed to be nothing he could do to remedy them.

On this autumn morning he was working alongside a group of men, combing the lawns with strong, long handled rakes to rid them of loose grass. He paused to rest his back which was often painful these days and saw his daughter walking up the terraces towards him, shading her eyes against the thin autumn sunlight which had little warmth in it. She raised a hand in greeting, smiling.

'What are you doing out here?' he asked accusingly, disconcerted by her sudden appearance. 'I woke you before I went out. You should be at work. You'll have missed your bus.'

'You forgot your flask. I brought it for you.'

She was a big girl, standing awkwardly, holding his flask over the fence. Her jeans and her rain jacket were too small for her, the jacket zipped up and clinging to heavy breasts, but much too thin for the day, the jeans too low slung. She embarrassed him. He loved her, but she made him uncomfortable.

'Put it down. Leave it there,' he said, quickly. 'I can't take it now, can I?'

'No. I'm sorry.'

She was always sorry. He felt compelled to say, 'Thanks for bringing it.' Even to himself his words sounded grudging, ungracious.

'No bother.'

'But why aren't you at work?'

'I was sick.'

'Were you? Are you alright?'

'I'm better now. Something I ate.'

She seemed very robust and healthy to him, an outdoor girl with apples in her cheeks. That was what her mother would have said. She was a tree in bloom, sturdy and handsome. All unconscious of the cold, she rubbed one foot up and down her leg, leaving a smear of mud on the denim. Mouse shy, she was afraid to go, afraid to stay.

He turned back to his raking and in doing so he noticed the other men watching Rosie with sidelong, covetous glances.

'Dad?'

'What?'

He looked over his shoulder and she was reminded of a horse, eyes wild, ears laid back.

Go away, just go away, he thought desperately.

'Nothing,' she said. 'I'll get off to work then. I texted them. Said I'd be a bit late.'

He watched her go back down the hill and shrugged in exasperation. He was not a bad man. The men who worked for him thought him very calm and quiet. He aroused no antagonism in them. His speech was gentle, with the occasional glimpse of an oblique, wry humour, which they appreciated. He was always tactful with strangers. Only with his daughter could he allow the mask of his civility to slip. It was at once a relief and an irritation to be with her.

She went back down the track to the cottage. She thought that she might as well go to work. When she looked in her purse to see if she had coins for the bus that passed the park gates, she was irresistibly drawn to the photograph in the card compartment. Several times a day, she found herself staring at it. It was a cheap mini print taken in a station booth. Her own face seemed large and vacant to her, like a full and witless moon. Her companion was a good looking boy with a clever, beaky face. He was screwing up his mouth and crossing his eyes for the camera. She remembered the sensation of his arm around her, fingers deftly squirming up inside her blouse, his too-long nails catching at the fabric, catching at her flesh.

'A nice warm girl,' he had said, chuckling in her ear. What was his name? Johnnie? Bobby? She had met him in a pub. She had been out with the girls from work. Somebody's hen night. A light summer night. At the end of the evening, she lost track of the others. The boy offered to walk her to the station so that she could get the train home. At the other end, she could have got a taxi back to the cottage. She had made sure she kept enough change to pay for it, following her father's instructions. He worried about her. But she didn't get on the train home. The boy persuaded her otherwise, kissing her, his tongue in her mouth. She had not taken much persuading. Besides, the last train had gone. What else could she do? It seemed exciting, daring. A grown up adventure. They ate burgers in the station and later, he took her to a club, an expensive place with good music, pink scented soap and hand cream in the ladies. She remembered all that, but she could not remember his name or where he lived.

He asked her if she wanted to come home with him. They took a taxi and she felt sick, but it was alright after a while. She wasn't sick. In his small flat with its debris of wet towels, cigarette ends, dirty clothes, her mind was fuzzy with unaccustomed alcohol, too happy, too overwhelmed by his welcome attention. Her body clung much too closely to this stranger. In the morning, he made her a cup of tea without milk, gave her paracetamol for her headache and walked her to the bus stop. 'The walk of shame,' he said, laughing at her flimsy dress, her naked legs, her too high heels. She remembered a busy city suburb with a newsagent on the corner, streets of old tenements interspersed with modern blocks, a bus shelter with a digital sign. Two minutes to the next bus. He waited with her, perched on the narrow seat, jiggling his foot up and down, up and down. He put her on the bus, telling the driver to let her out at the station, gave her a little peck on the cheek. His breath still smelled of cigarettes and whisky.

'I'll call you,' he said, waving her off.

Only later, she remembered that she hadn't given him her number and he had never asked for it. He had never even asked for her surname. The cool, ascetic face of her father came into her mind. She had told him that she had stayed overnight with a friend from work. He had assumed it was another girl.

'Why aren't you at work?'

Because I'm sick. Because I think I'm pregnant.

How could anyone manage to say such things? How could such things be? They must not be. She began to walk blindly around the little kitchen, her hands pressed to her temples as though something were hurting her there. He had carried her on his shoulders when she was small, showing her birds and trees and flowers. He had walked with his hands holding her small feet firmly, her fingers threaded in his hair. Her mother had been alive. She had been safe. How could she ever tell him? She stumbled against the table and banged her legs. Then she sat down and, resting her face in her hands, began to cry. Presently she washed her hot cheeks at the kitchen sink and dried her face on the tea towel, rubbing the colour back. She went out to catch the bus, walking up the long drive, letting the fresh air finally dispel the remnants of nausea. She was embarrassed. The driver might notice that she had been crying.

In the park, Martin raised his eyes to the birches. They were his favourite tree with their white papery bark, their drooping twigs that fashioned the springtime leaves into veils of coined light, a dazzling gold. And now they were golden again but with the deeper yellow of autumn. Rosie had been a gentle child. But adolescence had not favoured her. She had become clumsy, heavy and diffident. Even her name seemed too pretty for her solid, reproachful presence.

'I'm sorry,' she told him all the time. He had no sympathy for her. He no longer knew how to speak to her.

'These birches,' he said. 'They'll have to come down some time.

Getting past it.' The trees were so old that their bark had grown very dark, gnarled and irregular.

'Not much you can do with birches,' said one of his companions. 'They make good kindling. No heartwood though. One way and another, it's been a bad year for trees.'

Author's Note

This is a selection of my short stories written across a span of many years. In between times, I was busy working on plays, novels and non-fiction, but with a sizeable body of work in print, it seems like a good time to collect these together.

Most of them have been published in a variety of magazines and in one or two anthologies. These include the Other Voice, New Writing Scotland, Edinburgh Review, Word Magazine and Good Housekeeping.

Many thanks are due to the late Kenneth Roy, among others, for years of encouragement with my short fiction, and to Duncan Lockerbie at Lumphanan Press for invaluable assistance with this edition.

About The Author

Catherine Czerkawska is an extensively published writer of fiction (novels and short stories) popular non-fiction and award winning plays for theatre, BBC radio and television. Born in Yorkshire, of Polish and Irish parentage, she has spent most of her life in Scotland, with time also spent working in Finland, Poland and the Canaries.

Her novels include *The Physic Garden*, set in early nineteenth-century Glasgow, *The Jewel*, about the life and times of Robert Burns's wife, Jean Armour, both published by Saraband, and *The Amber Heart* and *Bird of Passage*, a powerful tale of cruelty, loss and enduring love, published by Dyrock Publishing. In 2019 Contraband published *A Proper Person to be Detained,* a family story that takes us from Ireland to the industrial heartlands of England and Scotland, giving voice to people often maligned by society and silenced by history – immigrants, women, the working classes. In 2023, Saraband will publish *The Last Lancer*, another personal account of loss and survival, this time in Poland and Ukraine.

Her stage plays include two full length plays commissioned by Edinburgh's Traverse Theatre: *Wormwood*, a play about the Chernobyl disaster staged in 1997 and Quartz. She has written plays for Glasgow's Oran Mor, as well as various community theatre projects, television drama and more than 100 hours of drama for BBC R4.

Her other interests include antique textiles, local and social history. She has served on the committee of the Society of Authors in Scotland and spent four years as Royal Literary Fund Writing Fellow at the University of the West of Scotland.

https://www.catherineczerkawska.co.uk/

Facebook: https://www.facebook.com/writerczerkawska/

www.ingramcontent.com/pod-product-compliance
Lightning Source LLC
Chambersburg PA
CBHW020740130626
46554CB00006B/2068